James H. Graff, Robert St. John Corbet

Sir Harry and the Widows

Nothing hazard, nothing lose - a love story, humorous and pathetic

James H. Graff, Robert St. John Corbet

Sir Harry and the Widows
Nothing hazard, nothing lose - a love story, humorous and pathetic

ISBN/EAN: 9783337383411

Printed in Europe, USA, Canada, Australia, Japan

Cover: Foto ©Andreas Hilbeck / pixelio.de

More available books at **www.hansebooks.com**

SIR HARRY

AND

THE WIDOWS:

OR,

Nothing Hazard, Nothing Lose.

A LOVE STORY, HUMOROUS AND PATHETIC.

BY

ROBERT ST. JOHN CORBET.

LONDON:

FREDERICK WARNE AND CO.

BEDFORD STREET, COVENT GARDEN.

NEW YORK: SCRIBNER, WELFORD, AND CO.

1868.

TO THOSE HONOURABLE MEMBERS OF THE HOUSE OF
COMMONS

WHO STROVE, ALAS! INEFFECTUALLY, TO PUT DOWN THE

PANDEMONIACAL NUISANCE

OF

𝕺rgan 𝕲rinding,

THE VERY TOOTHACHE OF NUISANCES,

SATAN'S REQUIEM FOR AUTHORS,

AND THE EAR-PLAGUE OF THE METROPOLIS,

𝕴 𝕯edicate this 𝕰ccentric 𝖁olume,

WITH INEXPRESSIBLE FEELINGS

OF GRATITUDE, ESTEEM, AND RESPECT.

SIR HARRY AND THE WIDOWS.

CHAPTER I.

FLOORED BY A WIDOW.

" MOTHER, I've half a mind to——"

" Harry, I do wish you would have a whole mind sometimes."

" So I will, dear mother; I will have my present one pieced. I want to speak to you on matrimonial subjects. A fellow cannot do better than consult his mother on these questions, because she has known what it is to have a fellow in love with her, and having taken notes of his sayings and doings, she can hand them down for her son's benefit. There are three goddesses imbibing nectar on my Olympus, and I am rather keen upon them all. Not that I care over much about them, you know, but I simply prefer them to the other millions in the world. First comes Lady Jemima Pooce, she——"

" Pooh! pooh! Harry."

" Down goes Lady Jemima's house. Well, how do you like Lady Hester Manson? It's all the same to me which I take."

" Lady Hester is much too old. A young man with such wonderfully high spirits as you possess; a man so essentially youthful, so untameable, so

B

mad, in fact, ought to choose a young, cheerful, sensible, merry girl. I know many mothers would prescribe a quiet, steady-going, prim young lady, with ultra-Evangelical tendencies, but I feel convinced that a good-hearted, lively girl is the best companion you could have; the one that would in the end make you the best wife, and tamer. She must be a good Church-goer."

"Hang it, dear mother, I go to Allhallows, Pearl Street, most regularly, and it's not my fault that there is no sermon at the four o'clock service!"

"Well, your wife must keep up this good practice and improve upon it. Now, I know a young lady who would prove herself perfection."

"Name."

"Nellie Branston."

"Nineteen, unaffected, inartificial, lively, plump, good-tempered, and thoroughly English. Yes, dear mother, I have half a mind——"

"Harry!"

"I mean a mind and a half to fall in love with her. Yes, I'll begin to-day. I'll take lessons in spooning; I'll read up love, and get somebody to coach me in sheepishness. By the way, mother, I heard something rather unpleasant at Bob Howard's last night: did it ever strike you that it would give my brother Gil very lively satisfaction to find that I had taken flight to a better world?"

"It would give him very lively *surprise*, I should think."

"Thank you, dear mother, thank you; a worse world, I ought to have said."

"What puts such ideas into your sadly empty head?"

"Sadly empty! ah! I like that: sadly empty!

yes, that is very good indeed. Well, Limmins told me."

"Mr. Limmins is a most disagreeable man, Harry, as wild as yourself, and not half so good-hearted or honest. If I wanted to make mischief I should tell Gilbert, and he would——"

"Hammer Limmins to death, and quite right too. I don't believe a word. Now I must be off; but, first of all, let me tell you that I have won over fifty pounds these last four evenings."

"Harry, Harry, I am ashamed of you! I thought you had given up playing for such large sums. Give the money to me."

"I confess I don't quite see that."

"Harry, give me the money. You have no right to spend money so won upon yourself. Come, I mean what I say."

"And so do I. *Au revoir,* fare thee well."

"Now give me the money, that's a good lad. I had four subscription cards this morning, and I want to give something handsome to each."

"I see, I see: well, mother, *your* head is not sadly empty, that's certain; but hang me, if mine wont be emptier than ever if I shell out as you wish. However, you shall have the tin when I come back. I see your game with half an eye— 'Lady Frankwell, twenty guineas,' 'Lady Frankwell, fifteen guineas,' &c. &c., and in each case the Duchess of Hallamshire's name with the usual empty-hearted, conventional two guineas opposite to it! Ha! ha! sadly empty! sadly empty! by Jove, I like that idea immensely! Ta, ta, mother mine. I will *revenons à nos moutons* at dinner."

Some young gentlemen are hustled into matri-

mony. A parent or guardian runs a pin into the
the youth, and says, " Now, you stupid lad, get a
wife." Whereupon the stupid lad rubs. his eyes,
and in course of time does his best to get a
wife by inaugurating a weak courtship, to be
followed up by a mild proposal. If he is accepted
—well and good. If rejected—serve him right.

Lady Frankwell had for some time been running
a pin into her son Sir Harry, but up to to-day its
point had had but little effect upon him.

Last night he had seen Lady Hester at the
Opera, and fancied she looked unusually pretty and
pleasant, and the following morning he had, as
we have read, spoken to his mother about her. To
her Lady Frankwell objected on the score of that
uncontrollable calamity, age, and then proposed
pretty Nellie Branston.

Sir Harry had known Nellie for years, for her
late father had held the living wherein the Frankwell property lay, for more than a quarter of a
century.

But Sir Harry had done no more than simply
admire the rector's pretty daughter ; he had not
once given Cupid a thought.

And as for Nellie, she had never allowed the
slightest suspicion of love to creep into her heart,
of love for young Harry Frankwell at least.

Cupid, however, *had* knocked at her heart ; but
Nellie, clothing herself with the instincts of John
Thomas, was a very long time in answering the
door.

It was in days of prosperity when Cupid knocked.
Then her father was rector of Dudsworth, and the
Toxophilite god was represented by a well-favoured
pupil, one Archibald Lorford by name.

This young gentleman had come to read with the rector for Oxford ; and right well though he stuck to his studies, he nevertheless found time to fall in love with his tutor's little daughter, a sturdy young lady in short frocks and long stockings.

He was matriculated with flying colours, being best of a batch of thirteen, and after boating and cricketing a term away, came back to Dudsworth to read during the Long. Time travelled on. Nellie's frocks grew longer and longer, till at length the stockings disappeared, and then she opened her pretty deep blue eyes, and then she began to take peculiar pleasure in the society of Archibald Lorford.

Now it so happened that Mr. Lorford and young Frankwell had never met ; the latter, much the younger of the two, was either at Eton, or visiting friends and relatives, when the former was at Duds-worth, or Mr. Lorford was himself visiting, or at Oxford when young Frankwell was at home. They did meet, however, as we shall see.

On the rector's death, Mrs. Branston and her children found themselves very badly off ; but their distresses were, to a great extent, relieved by the kindnesses, pecuniary and social, of Sir Gilbert and Lady Frankwell. In time also the two elder boys got something to do : one as clerk to a large London bookseller, the other as accountant in a brewery.

Archibald Lorford was abroad in the diplomatic service when the rector died, and it was some time ere he heard the sad news. He had not, indeed, heard anything of his old rector's family for several months, though the beauty of Nellie's face was seldom absent from his mind. Tired at length of

foreign service, he came home, resolved to make
the best in England of the four hundred a year
with which he was blessed. He took lodgings in
a village near Leeds, wherein Mrs. Branston was
now living with Nellie and her two youngest boys.

He became so desperately in love, that he could
see no rest in anything but matrimony. Though
he came to this conclusion in all seriousness, he
did not at once propose to pretty Nellie, because
he doubted his ability to keep two and contingencies upon a sum which he had found by no
means too much for one and the certainty of no
contingencies. Marry Nellie he certainly must;
but he must either be content to go through a
great deal of curtailing and drawing in of horns,
or increase the four hundred.

The latter idea seemed the preferable one, and
Archibald accordingly went up to London to call
upon the noble lord who had procured him his
diplomatic appointment. He expressed immense
affection for what is not usually looked upon as a
very paying concern—namely, the Civil Service;
but his affection was nipped in the bud by the
noble lord expressing great annoyance at Archibald's resignation of his diplomatic post, coupled
with a refusal to do anything more for so highly
unsatisfactory a *protégé*.

Archibald remained a fortnight in London, and
then returned to his old quarters. On calling at
Mrs. Branston's cottage, he learned that widow
and family had gone to London on a visit to Sir
Gilbert and Lady Frankwell; and then, of course,
ten thousand agonies possessed him, as he feared
that if young Harry did not fall in love with Nellie,
some other rich young fellow probably would.

It was but little attraction that life had now for Archibald Lorford, so desperately, and, as he fancied, so hopelessly, was he in love. However, he must await Nellie's return, and hope that she would bring back her heart amongst her other valuable goods and chattels.

Nellie did come back in time, and sooner than was expected, owing to the sudden death of Sir Gilbert Frankwell ; and just at the time too, most unluckily, when Archibald was staying with a great-expectation uncle in Scotland.

And she went back again after awhile to town to stay with a wealthy uncle, banker and M.P. ; and when Archibald, with heart beating, called at the cottage on his return home, he found it as good as empty. Verily this was " piling up the agony."

" Why was I such a fool," he exclaimed on walking away, " as not to try and make sure of her, and offer her the best home I could on four hundred a year ? I believe she loves me, and possibly she would marry me in the teeth of the mother, who is dying for her to make a good match, that she may be able to give the lads a lift."

Six weeks this second London visit lasted, and Nellie came in for a great deal of good company.

She cracked two hearts.

One belonged to a young Hampshire squire whom she refused ; the other to a nobleman's son who, unluckily, got scent of the brewery brother, and actually saw in broad daylight the other brother at the bookseller's desk !

" Connexion too shoppy !" with which remark the second admirer dismissed Nellie, though not without a real struggle.

At the end of the six weeks Nellie returned

home, and Archibald Lorford, who was then at his lodgings, picked up new life, and revisited the widow.

Ladies now and then, as we are well aware, entertain very strange notions, and of these strange entertainers Mrs. Branston was one. She had got it into her head that Archibald Lorford was a loose fish.

Never was man more maligned by woman since the Deluge.

One evening, drawing the blind aside to look at the state of the weather, Mrs. Branston had espied Archibald walking along on the opposite side of the road, and just as he was passing out of sight, he appeared to the widow to stumble, or rather to stagger.

" Tipsy," was the word on the tip of her tongue. Poor Archie! when a little boy he had sprained both his ankles, and they had never recovered their pristine strength, though they did their duty pretty well.

On this unlucky evening he had stepped upon a little round stone, and this gave his left foot a turn which was too much for the poor weak ankle. He staggered and nearly fell down. From this sprang the tipsy idea.

He smoked moreover, and cigars too, not pipes, a sure sign, according to the widow's creed, that he was not only loose but fast. He seemed also to have, at fewest, three hundred and sixty-five pairs of trousers, as Mrs. Branston felt sure that he never called in the same pair two days running. Mrs. Branston having given him a bad name, was of course determined to hang him. Archibald Lorford was a handsome, well-bred, well-dressed man, possessed of a good figure and good head, with a generally fashionable appearance, and all the manners and style of good society. He was in no way a loose fish, however.

The widow did not want him for a son-in-law, possibly because she was anxious to secure some one who would marry herself and sons, not Nellie only, and she gave her daughter a few hints as to the nature of her wishes. From hints she got to something more tangible, and one evening said, "I do not wish you to be cold, my dear, to Mr. Lorford, though I certainly should be pleased if something would happen to induce him to visit us less frequently. I want you to excuse yourself from singing so much for him. He can hear far better singing than yours at the music-hall in Leeds, and only praises you to please you, as so many fast men praise simple-minded country girls. I believe he thinks of nothing but eating and drinking, of smoking and new trousers, from morning to night."

Nellie said nothing; but, of course, from that moment she could not help loving Archie ten times more than ever.

Four days after, the widow re-introduced the subject, and wound up by telling Nellie plumply that if Mr. Lorford so far forgot himself as to propose, she was unconditionally to refuse him.

"Very well, mamma."

That was all Nellie said aloud; but her eyes told her pillow that night such a tale as I pray your pillow may never hear, my reader.

Nellie Branston was one of those noble girls who are perfectly willing to sacrifice themselves on the iron altar of Family Advantage. She very quickly guessed the reason of her mother's aversion to Archibald. She felt sure there was some one better off in her mother's eye. She had had a good rating for refusing the Hampshire squire, and she saw that her mother took the refusal so deeply to heart, that she resolved never to be what she called "undutiful" again.

When next the high priest attached to the altar of Family Advantage might be hard up for a victim, Nellie resolved to offer her services.

Believe me, my reader, she would be a pretty sacrifice, plump and without a blemish.

Mrs. Branston was convinced that Nellie might marry well, and being to some extent a woman of the world, she hoped to be elevated herself above that stage in society which has to be content with one maid-servant, and a grumbling charwoman on a Saturday.

Besides, there were two young boys to be provided for, one dying for the merchant service, the other pining for Australia, where he was under the impression that money was to be made. Verdant youth!

Young Frankwell, now Sir Harry, with nearly forty thousand a year, was very probably in the widow's eye.

Suddenly, Archibald was called away to nurse the great-expectation uncle in Scotland, and Mrs. Branston saw him not for four months. At the end of that time he was again in her little drawing-room, now irrecoverably in love with Nellie.

He had brought the widow some very acceptable presents from Scotland, and had obtained a half promise from a Glasgow merchant to take one of the boys into his office. All this had put her into a good humour, and for a week she seemed unaware that Archie was making most vigorous love to her daughter.

Archibald Lorford never made a greater mistake in his life than when he fancied, ten days after this, that he had " worked " the mother and got her " safe."

That mothers are to be worked and made safe, I do not deny ; but methinks, that much of the time occupied in working the mother would be much better spent upon the daughter.

Every one to his *goût*, however ; lookers on *don't* see most of the game of love !

But the young, fond hearts of pretty girls are not to be loosed when once they have got their teeth and claws into the happy victim. No ship of love made fast to the heart of an English girl ever yet dragged its anchors.

Convinced that he had the widow safe, Archibald Lorford tackled the mother, and most unfortunately chose the very worst time in the day for carrying out his design.

He chose the morning, which every one knows is the one time when ladies, who are not visible all day long, are most invisible. He came upon Mrs. Branston in her undress uniform : she was never more unsafe in her life : her one undress black stuff morning gown had to appear before a gentleman who possessed three hundred and sixty-four pairs of trousers, besides the apparently quite new ones he was at the moment wearing.

She was flustered and flurried.

She was somewhat more of a match for her visitor in an evening, that being the time he was usually expected, and then she was in receiving costume : at eleven o'clock in the morning, however, she was not in a position to receive cavalry of the calibre of Archibald Lorford.

He talked for half an hour in his quiet, pleasant, and fascinating way, and iced the widow, as he thought, before she had time to get warm.

In three quarters of an hour he begged leave to make open love to Nellie, faithfully depicting the depth of his affection for her, honestly stating that he had long been making quiet love to her, and firmly declaring that he believed Nellie's heart was perfectly ready to change places with his own.

I need waste neither your time nor mine in describing how the widow spun out her " No ! "

Archie got it, and of course he kicked at it, but it was too much for his weak ankles. He left the cottage.

" What a fool I was not to go straight to Nellie ! bother the woman, I thought I had her as safe as a house ! "

Off he started for Chelton Meadow, intending therein to cool and collect himself. In this very meadow, at this very time, it so happened that Nellie was walking with one of her brothers.

" Nellie, I declare ! " exclaimed Mr. Lorford, catching sight of the pretty girl. "I must and will speak to her."

Yes, sure enough he saw Nellie, accompanied by the brother with the English notion about Australia.

He soon came up with the brother and sister, and the former, who long since had seen his affection for Nellie, and moreover longed for Archibald as a brother-in-law, very sensibly pretended to look for mushrooms, and so left the pair to themselves.

Nervous though he was from his recent interview with the widow, Archibald nevertheless spoke to

Nellie in his usual way, quietly, pleasantly, and earnestly.

Of course he brought the conversation round to the subject of which his whole soul was full.

In half an hour he had stated his love, and *asked* Nellie to marry him.

Then he *implored* her.

Nellie's speech had been written for her, as we know, and the poor girl had simply to deliver it.

Again Archie and his poor weak ankles had to kick, Nellie herself plainly showing how easy it is to be choked by such unsubstantial trifles as words.

"Nellie, you do love me, I'm convinced you do, and nothing on earth shall keep us separate. We will be married, my darling girl, we will; we—— "

" No, no, no, Mr. Lorford."

"That's not your heart's answer, Nellie, and I wont take it. Nellie, my child, you are mine, you are, and I wont lose you. Such love as mine is not to be laid on one side quietly, for I am convinced that I have your heart, Nellie, and keep it I will, and enjoy it too. No one shall take you from me."

" Please not to talk to me more in this way, Mr. Lorford, I—I—I——"

Tears washed away the rest.

" Well, Nellie darling, I've no wish to distress you; it half kills me to see the tears in those darling eyes, though they tell me, yes, how plainly, that all the love I long for is, and yet must not be, mine. Nellie, your mother cannot keep us apart for ever; she cannot always hate me."

" She does not hate you, Mr. Lorford."

" Has she set her mind upon seeing you married to any one in particular? "

" I don't know."

" I can only account for her present aversion to me, after our long acquaintance, after the hundred and fifty kindnesses she has shown me, by believing that she hopes to marry you to some rich or influential man, to one who will marry the family, in fact. Nellie, will you be true to me? Will you keep your heart for me? I will not ask for it until I have found a home for you. Nellie darling, will you· be strong and firm? Will you be like scores of other girls who, through all opposition and a hundred unkindnesses, have kept their little hearts fast, and given them where only they could give all their love?"

Nellie had no reply: she could not repeat the speech her mother had written for her, and she could not declare her love.

The brother who had nominally been out mush-room-hunting, came to her relief by re-appearing at her side.

" Why, Nellie has been crying, Mr. Lorford," he said.

"Now, James, have you ever been told to hold your tongue?"

James confessed, with perfect truth, that he had.

" Well, I tell you again. Now don't you go blabbing at home about having seen your sister crying; remember to shut your mouth, and let this help you to refresh your memory," saying which, Archibald put two half-crowns into the boy's hand.

As they had not been standing still since they met, the trio had by this time nearly reached the end of the meadow, and were now but a few hundred yards from the widow's cottage.

Archibald walked with Nellie as far as he thought he might with prudence, and then made for his lodgings.

He was not all fears as may be supposed ; he was all hopes. Love so desperate as his knows no barriers. So long as Nellie remained in the village she was near him, and the knowledge of this was quite enough to floor all ideas of despair.

He would carry her off if need be ; the girl loved him ; of that he now felt convinced, so the idea of an insurmountable barrier to the realization of his wishes was ridiculous.

How he pitied the poor, dear, tender-hearted girl, shut up with one who had done her best to crush her youthful affections !

He had no language severe enough for Mrs. Branston, because he could see no reason whatever why Nellie's affections should not be allowed their own way.

The desperation of his love made him more than half wild, but it did not lead him to do anything actually violent. He did not rush up to Mrs. Branston's cottage, demand this or that, and, in fact, inflame the widow still more against him.

For hours, from the time he left Nellie, he walked up and down his room planning, unplanning, thinking, unthinking, and revolving a hundred ideas. He neither ate nor drank, nor did he swear, but he cried as only strong men cry who lose or woo in vain the Nellies of this see-saw world. Yet he was all hope, because he was all determination.

He cried for Nellie, not for himself only, for he was thoroughly convinced of her love for him, and thoroughly resolved was he to marry her some day by some means.

He little knew the kind of woman he had to deal with in Mrs. Branston.   Next chapter's events, however, taught him a little.

Strange to say he slept well that night, so well, indeed, that when he awoke, the events of the previous day came before his mind with an intensity and force of seeming reality almost equal to their original strength.   He had so utterly forgotten everything in a long, sound sleep, that, on awaking, he had a part of yesterday to go through again with all the bitterness of first pain.

Fortune favoured Nellie, for she did not see her mother for quite an hour after her parting with Archibald Lorford.   In this time all trace of weeping had an opportunity to take its departure, and she appeared before the widow unchanged in manner and appearance by the morning's trouble.

In the evening too she played and sang as usual, and read aloud a portion of the tale in the *Monthly Fulminator*, her mother's favourite publication, one apparently brought out with the charitable design of condemning to the lowest chambers of the uncomfortable world all persons who had the criminal audacity to be Tories and orthodox Churchmen.

How glad was Nellie to get to her own room; therein her pent up grief found relief, and heart-rending expression in bitter, bitter tears, and she almost cried herself into convulsions.

She had adored Archibald for years and years: he was this world's one attraction for her; his was the one breast on which she could have laid her head and felt more than happy.

And the day he told her his love was the very one on which she learned that she must lose him !

Poor Nellie !

Let no one think that I do not respect her feelings. Let no one believe me guilty of hard-hearted profanity if I quote the famous Byronic prescription for unhappy souls in her condition. I shall not offend Nellie, and I may benefit a broken-hearted reader.

> Ring for your valet: bid him quickly bring
>   Some Hock and soda water, then you'll know
> A pleasure worthy Xerxes the great king;
>   For not the blest sherbet, sublimed with snow,
> Nor the first sparkle of the desert spring,
>   Nor Burgundy in all its sunset glow
> After long travel, *ennui*, love or slaughter,
> Vie with that draught of Hock and soda water.

Love is the morning-star in the firmament of a clouded life; its brightness may now and then be obscured, but its light can never be wholly put out. Even as parting is such sweet sorrow, so is love too often such sweet pain. Love we must; yes,

> Let us have wine and sweethearts, mirth and laughter,
> Sermons and soda water the day after!

CHAPTER II.

SIR HARRY MAKES LOVE.

GENTLEMEN who go out in the world will tell you that they never knew a married lady yet who was not under the impression that she could see a great way through a brick wall; and the same gentlemen will add, that the good ladies, as a rule, singularly misjudge their ocular powers.

I don't think, however, that Mrs. Branston altogether misjudged hers, for she had a pair of singularly penetrative eyes.

On returning from her solitary afternoon walk she at once felt convinced that Nellie, who met her in the garden, had been crying, though there positively was not the trace of a single tear in either eye. Her penetration led her to feel sure that Nellie had met the ineligible lover, and that he had said something to her on the forbidden subject of love.

Ladies who really see a good way through brick walls don't talk much; they act. Mrs. Branston was true to this characteristic. That very evening she went to her landlord.

" I have come to give you the requisite week's notice," she said ; " and as I shall probably leave before the expiration of the week I have brought my rent with me, and shall be glad of a receipt."

Of course she gave some reason for this hurried departure, and on her arrival home took steps towards procuring other lodgings. She bethought her of old Lady Frankwell, and she bethought her of handsome Sir Harry.

He was fifty times handsomer, to her mind, than Archibald Lorford. For all the widow knew, he might have loved Nellie in the happy days of jackets and short frocks. Nellie's pretty face must necessarily bring up a thousand recollections of children's games and chatterings; he must have liked her when a boy, he must inevitably love her now a man.

The widow would try.

She would go up to London, nominally to be near her banker and M.P brother-in-law, and she would call upon Lady Frankwell in Cavendish Square with Nellie, and hope for invitations to dinner.

Sir Harry must fall in love with Nellie; he should not be allowed to help himself. And oh! the forty thousand a year! and oh, the prospect of getting Civil Service appointments for the two youngest boys! The widows eyes dilated, glistened, and were ablaze with hope and anticipations!

Mrs. Branston at once wrote to London to the owner of the apartments she had occupied on her last visit to the metropolis, and begged that, if unlet, they might be got ready for her. She was a Colin Campbell in her smartness and readiness of action.

When Archibald Lorford awoke the next morning, he resolved to visit the widow in the course of the day; but hour passed hour, and the requisite courage, or whatever the quality might be, failed him.

Folks talk, neither prettily nor properly, of moving Heaven and earth to do this, that, and the other thing ; Archibald Lorford would be quite satisfied if he could move one little, plain, disagreeable woman. Such a girl as Nellie must not be lost without a terrific struggle ; but he must struggle to some extent gently, for Mrs. Branston was only a woman.

" Only a woman !"

Poor Archie ! he little knew the sex when he gallantly put in this addendum ! Wags say that the hardest key to turn is a donkey ; let them try to turn a woman, and then let them say which is the harder !

In the course of the afternoon, Archibald felt able to set out to tackle Mrs. Branston.

I confess he felt a little nervous as he walked along, though he was fully aware that the enemy was only a widow ; she, however, was in possession of the fortress, and nine points of the law, moreover, were in her favour, inasmuch as she was in full possession of Nellie.

Only let Archie get sufficiently near Nellie to whisper that little word " elope," and the widow's seeming advantages would be scattered to the wind.

Archibald was very desperate. He would think nothing of proposing an elopement ; and if Nellie could but shelve her conscience for five minutes, and beg, borrow, or steal a little courage, he believed that she would run off with him.

Opportunities for eloping don't come with ceaseless watchings and waitings ; they start up almost when least expected. Moreover, they are only for the Colin Campbells of the world, for the hot-iron strikers ; the Fabii Cunctatores would be nowhere in an elopement.

Archibald was now on his way to the cottage. The widow was at her bed-room window darning a stocking.

Presently she started; she had evidently seen some thing or body; down went the stocking upon the floor, down went the widow into the kitchen.

"Martha, I see Mr. Lorford coming here; don't let him in; don't say I'm out, but say that I don't wish to see him again."

A few minutes after these orders were given, Archie knocked at the door. Martha went to open it, the widow following, and posting herself so that she would be hidden when the door was opened.

" Is Mrs. Branston at home ?"

" Yes, sir, but she don't want to see you."

" Does not want to see me ?   Oh, nonsense !   I wont detain her five minutes."

" Missis told me not to let you in, sir."

" Why, I wonder ?   I must see her; I must indeed just for a minute;" and Archie got on to the top step, and lifted up his right foot with the intention of setting it down in the passage.

He was prevented, for the widow, unseen, pushed the door out of Martha's hand, closed it in Archibald's face, and locked it.

What did he do then ?

Why, he went round to the back door.

The widow was too much for him here; for she too went there, and by a shorter route, locked the door, ay, and clapped the shutter up.   He was done.

There was no doubt about that; and quiet and gentlemanlike though Archibald usually was in his language, this was an opportunity which the devil could not let slip, and Satan made him swear.

Sir Harry Frankwell would have eased himself in this manner long ago; not, however, that I wish you to regard him as such an utter vagabond as gentlemen with a red hand are popularly represented in print. He certainly was, as we shall find, somewhat of a loose fish, fast, slangy, and extravagant; but on no account would his name be admitted amongst the F's in the Baronetage peculiar to the *London Journal* and the Victoria Theatre!

If you were to ask Archibald what he did on finding the back door closed and shuttered, he would be utterly unable to tell you.

He was in no condition to make notes. How he got from the house to his own lodgings he could never remember; he did arrive, certainly, for on coming to his senses he found himself lying on his own sofa.

Now Mrs. Branston could tell you all she did. First of all she called Nellie.

"Fenella,"—she always used the baptismal name in full canonicals when feeling sour,—"pack up your boxes at once, and help James and Henry. We shall leave for London by the 1.10."

And Mrs. Branston and family did leave by the 1.10, which, being a truly rural train, started at 1.50, and late in the evening the widow was in her old London lodgings.

These lodgings happened to be in Mortimer Street, Cavendish Square, and as the Frankwell town house was 53, Cavendish Square, it will be evident that they were faultless in the matter of situation.

Next day, Mrs. Branston called upon Lady Frankwell, and sat an hour. The day following, the call was returned, her ladyship taking out the widow and Nellie for a drive, falling, at the same time, deeply in love with the latter, who had become a girl of wonderful perfections.

"Come to dinner to-morrow, my dear Mrs. Branston, and bring Fenella with you. Harry is at home, and will be delighted to see you, I am sure."

And during these twenty-four hours, Lady Frankwell settled to her own satisfaction how extraordinarily delightful it would be if Nellie could but captivate her mad-cap, harum-scarum son Harry.

She wanted sadly to settle him, and had long been on the look out for a good wife.

Knowing Nellie's character, and now becoming aware of her wondrous beauty as a grown up girl, Lady Frankwell felt that there was no one she had yet seen so likely to tame and humanize her affectionate, but terribly wild son.

And during these twenty-four hours, the other widow, Mrs. Branston, came to pretty much the same conclusion.

Mrs. Branston and Nellie came to dinner, and Harry admired the latter immensely. For two or three days Sir Harry made no remark about Nellie, but like the immortal parrot, he thought a good deal.

In a week's time Nellie was brought upon the *tapis*, as we have seen at the beginning of the first chapter, and Sir Harry settled to make love to her.

That same afternoon he called upon the widow and won her heart in a second.

"Just the heart I don't want to win," he observed to himself.

He mentioned the fact of this visit to his mother.

"And I do wish you would fall really in love with the daughter, stupid lad."

"Gently, mother, gently. I must take my time about it; recollect that my head is a sadly empty one. A fellow must have a few brains, even for making love."

Sir Harry was desperately in love now with Nellie.

"She's such a thoroughly English girl, mother. No die-away, swoon-away, super elegant, twaddling specimen of humanity; she's all sense, all strength, all beauty, all health, all Englishness."

Then he argued with himself day after day, that gloriously delightful though bachelorhood was, matrimony with Nellie would be only bachelorhood under another name, and a million times more delightful than what he was enjoying at present.

Such a girl as Nellie would see no harm in billiards, Champagne, or shilling cigars. *She* would glory in Epsom, Newmarket, Ascot, and Doncaster. *She* wouldn't abuse Limmins, and Graham Menzies, Lord Huntingsdale, Bob Howard, and jolly fellows like *them*.

Oh, no; Nellie would be a regular bachelette herself, and he would teach her billiards, skating, and how to make a glove-book on the Derby, and she should learn to shoot too, and begin by blazing away at the weather-cock over the stables at Dudsworth.

Sir Harry grew more enthusiastic day after day, and long before he proposed, gave out to the jolly fellows of his set that he was going to be married.

"Whew-w-w-w-w-w-w-w!" was the unanimous exclamation that followed the announcement.

" Fact, I assure you."

" To whom ?"

" To a girl !"

" Probably : name ?"

" Oh, dear no ; name altogether too sacred."

" Well, let's drink her health."

" By all means."

" Pretty ?"

" I believe you, Bob : we shall be the handsomest couple out."

" Well, tell us something about her."

" Well, she's nineteen, sensible, unaffected, thoroughly English, five feet five and a half, likes billiards——"

" No ?"

" Well she *looks* as if she likes them ; means to back Snuffbox for the Leger; understands shooting, skating, fishing, riding, swims like a top—like a fish I mean—plays divinely, leaves Adelina nowhere in singing, thinks Cabanas perfectly delicious, hates poetry, awfully fond of the theatre, been up Mont Blanc——"

" No ?"

" Well, she looks as if—no she doesn't, she's not such a fool as to walk up hill to her grave with her eyes open; paints; read Bon Gaultier right through."

And on, on, on in this strain would Sir Harry extol Nellie, inventing accomplishments and achievements for her till he was nearly hoarse.

Notwithstanding his boundless enthusiasm, Sir Harry conducted his love-making in a most quiet and orderly manner.

How the widow's eyes glistened as he fidgeted for the first few days, evidently so unused to the undertaking as to feel not unlike a salmon on a gravel walk! He was evidently in love; how the widow's eyes glistened!

Good bye, one maid-servant! Good-bye, grumbling charwoman of Saturday! Good-bye, shoulder of mutton a thousand times hashed! Good-bye, ribs of beef inevitably minced!

How the widow's eyes glistened!

Sir Harry got on capitally after the first four days; presents poured in upon Nellie; invitations to dine at 53, Cavendish Square, arrived faster and faster; Sir Harry tried hard to win.

He was no bad fellow; he was worth the love even of such a girl as Nellie. He certainly was wild, rackety, and frivolous; he played cards a good deal, and always for money; he imbibed Champagne freely, rather too freely; he swore now and then, and was desperately slang.

I don't think I have anything worse to say of him. He was only twenty-four years of age now, and doubtless would improve, like his port.

After three weeks of ecstatic love-making, he proposed.

Poor Nellie! how could she be expected to listen to a proposal from him, with her head brimful of Archibald Lorford?

The high priest attached to the altar of Family Advantage was at her elbow during these three un-happy weeks, and a dozen times each day was he called upon to make his presence known.

One afternoon, Nellie, in the depth of her despair, actually told the widow that she could never love Sir Harry; that ——. She could get no further.

The look the widow gave her was something

awful; Nellie burst into tears of bitterness, into such tears as do sometimes flow from the eyes of those who ought to know nothing but the brightness that sparkles up from a happy heart.

It is true the widow was moved, but, like an elastic band, she returned, when loosened, to her original state.

She gave Nellie one look: she spoke one sentence, but this was enough. The united Universities could not have told the poor girl more.

Nellie in a second recollected herself; in a second the altar of Family Advantage rose up before her; in a second she threw herself upon it, resolved to fulfil the sacrificial office to the last cinder.

Four days after this came the proposal.

"Don't ask me now, Sir Harry, I cannot give you an answer indeed," she said.

Sir Harry was astonished: he could be a very quiet fellow when he liked, and he was at all times a considerate one, so he asked no questions, and left Nellie to herself.

His mother, knowing what was to happen that day, awaited his return, not with any fear as to the result of the proposal, but nevertheless a little anxiously.

" Well, Harry, what's the news ?"

" Left sitting : at least, adjourned *sine die.*"

" Why, my dear boy, you've not been re——"

" Oh ! dear no, not rejected nor refused, nor re——, whatever you call it; simply not accepted. I must go and see Graham Menzies ; he was not accepted once. I shan't be back to dinner, dear mother."

And off Sir Harry went.

He did not visit Nellie for three days, probably at the suggestion of Captain Menzies, and on the fourth he entered her presence somewhat nervously.

Nellie's kind reception soon nerved him, and to him she seemed more cheerful, more agreeable, more fascinating than ever.

The widow had caught scent of the demi-refusal, and no doubt she had *looked* at Nellie.

There was no standing the gaze of those eyes, which could travel a good way through a brick wall.

The gaze had been backed up with an entreaty, and certainly the widow put the family case in a light of such dazzling strength as would have thrown into the shade many a powerful appeal on behalf of a big scoundrel at the Old Bailey.

Let Nellie think of the condition of her mother and brothers now ; let her picture what it would be if she were the wife of forty thousand a year.

Family Advantage made Nellie a most accomplished feigner.

Convinced that her love had lost all its neutral tint, that it was now deep and real, Sir Harry, after ten days more of enthusiastic worship, a second time proposed. When, after stating, and right honestly and powerfully too, the depth of his own affection, Sir Harry said—" Dearest, dearest Nellie, do you love me ?" the poor girl hung down her head and made no reply.

When, however, ten seconds after, he said— " Darling Nellie, will you marry me ?" the widow's daughter timidly, and in a musically low voice, answered " Yes."

Four days after, the *Morning Lamp Post* " believed that a marriage had been arranged between Sir Harry Frankwell, Bart., of Dudsworth Castle,

Hampshire, and Ledgington Park, Salop, and Miss Fenella Millicent Branston, only daughter of the late Rev. J. D. Branston, formerly Rector of Dudsworth."

And a copy of that *Morning Lamp Post* fell under the eyes of Archibald Lorford, Esq., M.A. Oxon.

CHAPTER III.

ARCHIBALD LORFORD IN THE LITTLE BACK GARDEN.

FOR a fortnight after the closing of the back door, and the putting up of the shutter, Archibald Lorford had been in the doctor's hands.

A man cannot love so desperately as did he, and not be all the better or worse for it : there is no *via media* in such cases.

The day following the unceremonious refusal of admittance into the widow's abode, Archibald had ventured upon a second visit, hoping for better things, fully determined to secure Nellie somehow or other, and bear her off.

The widow, as we know, was gone.

He had a long parley with the hungry charwoman who opened the door, and could learn nothing from her as to the direction of the widow's flight. In a few minutes, however, the woman, on catching sight of a half-crown in Archibald's palm, invented a direction and even destination, telling him that she believed, but couldna' say for sartin, that Mrs. Branson had gone to a cousins at Yarmouth.

She received the half-crown, and Archibald wasted three days among the bloaters, seeing nothing, of course, of his angel.

The excitement, the disappointment, the desperation of his love, and half a dozen other little matters, now conspired together, and Archibald found himself so ill that he was obliged to send for a doctor, and submit to medical dictation for a fortnight.

From Yarmouth he went, on his recovery, to London, and spent a week there, chiefly in the neighbourhood of Nellie's uncle's house, wherein he thought the object of his boundless love might now be staying.

He never caught a glimpse of her, and being utterly unable to discover her present whereabout, hurried off to the Continent, and passed a month in travelling.

It was at Vienna that he saw an old copy of the *Morning Lamp Post,* the one announcing the "arrangement" of Sir Harry's marriage.

How he got through the next week it were little less than impossible to say: he did survive it, and suddenly astonished the waiters and all who knew him, with an extraordinary display of vivacity and nervous excitement. Of which this paragraph was the cause:

" We understand that the marriage of Sir H. K. Frankwell, Bart., and Miss Branston will be celebrated with full choral service, on Thursday next, the 14th inst., at Allhallows, Pearl Street."

Archibald Lorford threw down the paper as though it were on fire, rushed up to his bed-room, instantly packed his portmanteau, demanded his account, paid it, and was safe in the train making the best of his way home.

Like the widow, he was a Colin Campbell in smartness. At four o'clock on the afternoon of Wednesday the 13th, he was in London at Bacon's Hotel, and but a few minutes after he was in Cavendish Square reconnoitring number 53.

In about an hour's time, a handsome drag, drawn

by four fine bays, was tooled into the square, and, stopping at 53, discharged three ladies— Lady Frankwell, Mrs. Branston, and Nellie, in fact; and two gentlemen—Sir Harry, and his best-man-elect, Lord Huntingsdale.

Was Nellie to be married from Lady Frankwell's house, and not from that of her banker uncle or from the widow's lodgings?

This question Archibald put to himself, and rightly concluded that the wedding would be from number 53.

The banker uncle had offered his house, and invited Nellie and the widow there; but Lady Frankwell, who insisted upon doing everything herself, had taken the widow and daughter from their lodgings, and settled them in her own house.

Therefrom Nellie was to be married to-morrow morning at Allhallows, Pearl Street.

Nervously and anxiously Archibald Lorford serenaded Nellie for two hours that night. Once he fancied he saw her at what he guessed to be her bed-room window, and once he fancied he beheld the widow there.

All, however, was fancy.

He had not come from Vienna to London for nothing, we may be sure; he must have one more look at Nellie before she was lost to him for ever.

Now it so happened that Lady Frankwell's house was well known to him, for her ladyship's father had bought it from his great-expectation uncle; of this fact Archibald meant to take advantage.

Often and often had he stayed in the house as a boy during his uncle's ownership, and there was no part of it with which he was not acquainted;

amongst other things, he knew the way into the little back garden, a route somewhat intricate.

It would be too late, and, in fact, would half kill Archibald to see Nellie in Church ; he must see her while she was wholly and entirely Nellie *Branston.* He had only one chance of getting this view and of being unseen himself, and that was by working his way through the mews into the back garden. A very snug little room had its one window looking on to this garden, and if the door were but mercifully open, Archie would be able to see into the hall, and also catch a glimpse of the door of a morning room, which he thought might very probably be the private apartment of widow and daughter.

Archibald returned to the hotel to think the night away.

Vastly excited was Harry Frankwell at the prospect of his marriage.

He loved Nellie he knew not how much, and felt certain that he would be immensely happy with her.

He had made her most handsome presents since he proposed ; he had to a great extent given up the use of emphatic language ; he had not been in the least degree under the vinous influence of his favourite widow, Madame Clicquot ; nor had he played cards for any great sums, merely what he called " mild whist, bob points."

He had paid in a very handsome sum to the widow's account in her brother-in-law's bank, and had given the four boys a thousand pounds each. The brewery and bookseller brothers were now clerks, thanks to Sir Harry, in the bank of Messrs. Tutt, Dangett, & Co., the third boy was to go into the navy, and the youngest to be crammed for Sandhurst.

"Damme, I've done the handsome, Hunty," Sir Harry observed to Lord Huntingsdale; and verily, he spoke truth.

What now of Nellie?

Her feelings were truly such as defy accurate and comprehensive description.

She had had a cruel time of misery since the day of the proposal; and oh! how earnestly, how eagerly had she longed for but one turn in the wheel of fortune, which might bring Archibald Lorford near to her, near enough for her to rush to him, and be carried away she cared not whither.

To lose Archie was half death to her; but to be obliged to marry a man whom she could not love was more than death.

Nellie suffered intense, indescribable misery, and it was wonderful how she got through every day, seeing that on no one night since the proposal had she slept for longer than two hours.

Every day she had to be merry, acting under the orders of the grim high priest, and profess wondrous enjoyment in going with Lady Frankwell and Sir Harry to theatres, to dinner parties, and similar excitements. She had to receive magnificent presents with smiles; and since her engagement, to submit to that horrible species of sacred enjoyment, made more than ever famous by Arditi's *Il bacio* valses.

Now this species of sacred enjoyment, so delicately hinted at, is very tolerable and pleasant when there is plenty of love afloat. Nobody in the world thought it more tolerable than our friend Sir Harry; to Nellie, however, the sacred enjoyment was like the spike in the frog's back. What was fun to the schoolboy spiking was death to the frog spiked; what was fun to Sir Harry's enthusiastic lips was agony to sweet Nellie's.

Of course Sir Harry took for real appreciation all Nellie's feigned good graces in the matter of engaged kisses. He knew nothing of her love for Archibald Lorford; the widow had kept this quite in the dark, for she knew that Sir Harry was far too good a fellow to play the rival if he felt that the original wooer had a good chance, rivalry apart, of being a winner.

The two widows had had a short conversation on the subject, and Mrs. Branston had lyingly told Lady Frankwell that she did not believe Nellie cared for Archibald Lorford now. She said that her daughter preferred him to Sir Harry when she was quite a girl, but that she had no thought of anybody but Sir Harry now. Herein she lied, and, as we shall find, bitterly repented of her wilful inaccuracy ere long. Lady Frankwell made a note of all the widow said, but was too much wrapped up in the idea of Harry finding a tamer in Nellie to pay any attention to Archibald Lorford's pretensions.

Poor Nellie! she was to be married to-morrow morning.

Not one single minute did she sleep the night previous, and Archibald Lorford enjoyed exactly the same amount of repose.

Sir Harry sat up with Lord Huntingsdale till one o'clock in the morning.

"It's that infernal speech I shall have to make at the breakfast that floors me, Hunty"

"Well, it needn't: do as my military brother Dick. He got up, said 'Thank you,' and then

compared his bride to a post, saying that if anybody
wanted him at any time he was sure to be found,
like a good soldier, at his post !"

" Damme, that was downright clever : I'll do
exactly the same thing, though I should like to say
what I think of my wife, you know."

" Rubbish ! how can you when you know nothing
of her ?   It is not until a man has been married
about a year that he begins to find out whether his
partner · is a good, bad, or indifferent wife.   Ten
thousand girls are glorious creatures to talk, laugh,
dance, or walk with, but oh ! Harry, matrimony
sometimes makes them horses of quite another
colour.   Harry, my boy, matrimony is an awful
risk ; it beats twelve per cent. into fits !"

" Confound you, Hunty, what the deuce do you
mean by telling me this ?   Why Nellie's a goddess,
an Ethiopian, to speak allegorically—no, I mean
metaphorically, who can't change her spots."

" Skin, you mean."

" Yes, and—and—and——"

" Now, Harry, don't get excited : matrimony
does make the fair sex change."

" No doubt, Hunty, and for the better, of course."

" No, no.   I never met a married man yet who
did not tell me that the happiest time of his life
was——"

" The honeymoon ?"

" No."

" The day the son and heir was born ?"

" No."

" The day his mother-in-law died ?"

" No.   The few weeks or months of the engagement."

Sir Harry took another glass of Moselle.

" Hunty, do me a favour ?"

" With pleasure."

" Just bring me into the presence of the married men you allude to, that I may have the satisfaction of breaking their necks."

Soon after this the friends parted for the night, Sir Harry not a little uncomfortable when he thought that he might be just ending instead of beginning the happiest days of his life !

The uncomfortableness vanished when he took down a handsome photograph of Nellie and placed it before him.

" Such a girl as *that* change her spots ! no, no, no ; don't believe it. She's all right, and there are hundreds like her ; hundreds in England, if not anywhere else."

And he went to bed happy, and passed a night of most vigorously refreshing slumber.

On the day appointed for Nellie's wedding, Archibald Lorford was up early, and he was out of doors early too.

He dodged about in front of the house in Cavendish Square, a little afraid of being seen, because if Mrs. Branston were sleeping in the blue-room she might very possibly spy him were she to look out of the window.

If Nellie had but seen her matutinal serenader, I am convinced that she would have walked down stairs, let herself out at the front-door, and have thrown herself, almost literally thrown herself, into Archie's arms.

Her mind was a volcano of burning, fiery, raging misery. The anticipation of being married to Sir Harry, good fellow though he was, almost maddened, almost distracted her.

At times she felt determined that she would not go away with him; that she would stay with her mother, little cause though she had to love her at the present time.

But it was useless coming to any but one determination—namely, to sacrifice herself, as so many have, on the iron altar of Family Advantage.

Nellie cried not, for tears would not come, and whilst she felt that her heart was breaking, she felt too that there was no chloroform of even temporary comfort at hand, that a few hours must complete and consummate her misery.

After breakfasting, Archibald Lorford walked to Allhallows Church and inquired when the choral wedding was to be performed.

At a quarter past eleven.

At exactly five minutes to eleven Archie entered Cavendish Square for the second time that morning, and went round into the mews. He gently raised the latch of the third door he came to, and entered a little court. Evidently well acquainted with the *ambages viarum,* he chose a path that led to the right, and in another half minute was in the little back garden. The window of the little room was open, but the door was closed.

Was there no chance of seeing Nellie?

Had she been already dressed, and was she waiting for the carriage downstairs?

If he could summon up enough courage to step into the little room, and open the door, he might see her were she in the hall or the morning-room.

There was no *if* in the matter.

He crept into the room, and——

Footsteps outside warned him back, and caused him to retreat behind a straggling bush in the garden.

Was he too late ?

He dared not have come earlier, because in his uncle's time this little room was devoted to breakfast when the family in the house did not consist of more than four. Lady Frankwell very probably breakfasted there now, with Sir Harry, the widow, and Nellie.

Archibald perspired with the intensity of his anxiety, with the desperate idea that this was the sole chance, if chance it were, of seeing his own good angel—his long loved Nellie *Branston*.

Nellie FRANKWELL—he went cold at the idea. Did ever lover build upon more slender hopes? Who but a lover would think that there was the very weakest chance of the girl he was dying to see coming into a little back room on her wedding morning ?

What should bring her there, he could not say. At all events he dared watch nowhere else, and here he had a good reason for staying, independently of its being the best concealed place about the house.

On the table he spied, when he got into the room on his venturesome errand of opening the door, a pair of white gloves, and by their side a handsome gold scent bottle.

Could these be Nellie's ?

The gloves certainly looked more than $6\frac{1}{4}$, Nellie's size, as he was very well aware ; but on the top of the scent bottle he could plainly see the letters " F. F." elegantly inlaid ; could these stand for anything but " Fenella Frankwell ?"

Hope assured him that they could stand for that, and that only.

If he had but reflected a minute, he would have

remembered that Lady Frankwell's name, the name
of the dowager elect, was Frances.

But he did not reflect; hope raised him beyond
the realms of reflection, the intoxicating spirit of
that hope of which, if man were deprived, not a
hundred Registrars-general could take note of the
daily suicides throughout the land. Such hope
kept Archie going these moments of anxious sus-
pense.

Nellie was upstairs being dressed, her new maid
perpetually speaking to her as "my lady."

She was not to be attired, as if for an evening
ceremony, in candle-light costume, but in a handsome morning dress of rich fawn-coloured silk,
most exquisitely adorned as to body and skirt.

The rest of her attire was of the best and costliest
description, showing too the highest perfection of
good taste in every single particular.

A more adorably fascinating bride never entered
a Church.

Nellie looked superbly lovely.

She was blessed with a most exquisitely perfect
form, the contour of the upper part of her figure
being of faultless symmetry. She was tall too,
and more graceful than any swan that ever yet sang
and died. Her complexion was as pure as a pearl,
her deep blue eyes, her rich light brown massive
hair, together with that most charming of all attrac-
tions, a rosy, healthy English colour, rendering her
face such an one as picture never yet represented—
such an one as never yet existed but on the shoulders of Fenella Branston.

Nellie, to all appearance, was wonderfully composed; in fact, so thoroughly composed as to astonish
her maid, who thought that a bride elect ought to

look very happy, and be merry, and be very particular about being set off to the best advantage in her wedding attire.

Not a word scarcely did Nellie speak whilst being dressed; she left all to the maid. Had the latter thought of putting her bracelets on her knees Nellie would not have objected, or gone so far as to suggest that they would be seen to more advantage on her wrists.

In a very short space of time she was quite ready, and without even giving a farewell look in the glass came downstairs.

Sir Harry and Lord Huntingsdale were on their way to church, and of course Graham Menzies, Mr. Limmins, Bob Howard, and twenty other jolly fellows were there already. There were, it was said, eight orthodox parsons in the vestry. The Church was over crammed, three ladies actually appropriating the pulpit; there were three men instead of two to blow the organ, and despite the fact of its being a week day, six men choristers had put in an appearance.

Lady Frankwell was just leaving her room most handsomely dressed, as was her wont, and Nellie's mother was ready, with the exception of her hands, the gloves for which could not be found in any one of the eighteen drawers in her room. She perspired from head to foot; it took very little to fuss her when she was in a hurry or anxious to be particularly composed. When she was engaged in anything she liked, no matter how difficult, for instance in out-generaling Archibald Lorford, then she was all composure, all *qui vive*-ness, prepared for any reverse, and altogether unable to be put about. Now she was horribly flustered, just as she was when Archie called upon her one morning, she in a stuff gown, he in his three hundred and sixty-fifth pair of trousers.

"Oh, I remember," she suddenly exclaimed, and off she went downstairs.

All anxiety was Archibald Lorford as he crouched behind the bush. Presently the door of the little room was opened.

How his heart beat!

He heard the noise as of the rustling of a silk dress, and cautiously peeped through the leaves.

Ten thousand horrors, it was the widow!

Having taken her gloves from the table, she left the room, closing the door.

Poor Archibald! his heart sank within him. But it began to beat very vigorously in less than a minute, for the door was re-opened, and the rustling of silk again sounded in his ears.

"If Miss Branston is ready, Percome, tell Biggs that I will have the carriage at once. I left my scent bottle in the breakfast-room, just get it for me. Oh, you are here, Nellie dear, bless you! Kiss me, my child, the carriage will be ready directly."

"Very good, Lady Frankwell," replied Nellie.

How Archibald strained his eyes to catch a glimpse of the speakers, for their voices were plainly audible as Lady Frankwell's maid opened the door to get the scent bottle.

All in vain! the eager lover saw the maid, but no Nellie. The door was closed, and then his heart seemed not only to sink but to vanish.

"I shall not see her," and he almost cried in the agony of prospective disappointment.

In a second, he resolved to brave all dangers, to

run all risks, boldly to open the door and enter the hall.

What might not Nellie do if she saw him? Might she not rush to him? Might he not even save her whilst in the enemy's fortress? Had he not come purposely to save her?

Nothing venture, nothing win; if he hazarded nothing, he would be sure to lose everything.

He crept to the window.

But in a second he crept back, for he heard the sound of the door handle being turned.

For the third time the door was opened, and for the third time a daughter of Eve entered the room.

How his poor fluttering heart beat now!

Oh! that he might now prove the truthfulness of Tom Moore's Muse, when she sang—

> When once the young heart of a maiden is stolen,
> The maiden herself will steal after it soon.

CHAPTER IV.

TOO MUCH FOR THE WIDOW.

YES, how his poor heart did beat as he caught sight of a figure which certainly belonged to neither of the widows. How the man's heart did beat, ay, as though by steam! how the perspiration started from pore after pore! how his great brown eyes made themselves necks, and strained themselves well nigh out of their sockets! The figure was too tall to be that of Lady Frankwell, and was totally different in construction to that of Mrs. Branston.

It was Nellie whom Archibald Lorford saw before him, the one sole Nellie of any note that this world possessed.

On coming downstairs Nellie had felt faint, and she accordingly made at once for the little breakfast-room, well knowing that a bottle of strong salts was always kept upon the chimney-piece therein.

She took two or three exhaustive sniffs, and feeling better turned to leave the room.

So surely as some grief is speechless, so surely as there are times of sorrow when tears will not flow, so surely are there times when there is a partial suspension of reason, when ordinary locomotion, the going about to do this and that is little more or less than mechanical.

For the last three weeks Nellie had eaten and drunk, talked, laughed, walked, and listened by a species of mechanism that had taken the place of reason, and appetite, of lingual, locomotive, and auricular power. The dreadful thought of this contemplated marriage had upset her senses, and almost blunted the edge of her understanding. She had not of course lost consciousness, but was half paralysed with wretchedness.

For days and days she had been in this state, even though she maintained a kind of feeling which was meant for resignation. She had become such an accomplished feigner, that she was able to carry any amount of mechanical merriment about her in company; but this crowning act, this climacteric, this ceremony of marriage so soon to be performed, was testing her feigning powers to the uttermost. It was indeed only by machinery that she could exist now. Hers was wretchedness that has oft indeed been undergone, but one that it would require a new language, new descriptive powers, to portray.

Mechanically she turned to leave the room.

The idea that she was about to go and pass away from him seemed to arouse Archibald and wake him into action.

" Nellie, Nellie !"

She turned round, and stopped.

The voice soon took the mechanism out of her.

" Nellie."

She rushed forward, and in a second was in Archibald's arms.

Was she in time? had she been seen? was this last thought of, this utterly *un*-thought of cup of hope, to be shattered to a thousand pieces ere she raised it to her lips?

" Oh, save me, save me !" she cried, as she clung

to him who alone in this world could really save
her.

"Save you, Nellie?" he said, as he clasped her
tightly. "Save you?"

The iron was hot, now or never must he strike.
Would he be Colin Campbell or Fabius Cunctator?

"Save you, my child—I WILL!"

He raised her from the ground, carried her in
his arms, took her down the garden, through the
mews, unseen by half a dozen grooms, and hailing
a cab, luckily at the moment passing, placed her
therein, seated himself beside her, and gave orders
to be driven to a spot about two hundred yards
from Paddington Station. He was too much for
the widow this time!

Nothing venture, nothing win.

*   *   *   *
*   *   *   *

The widow's intellect was far too dense to allow
of anything flashing upon it, as the truth is said to
flash sometimes.

Ten minutes had passed, and there were no signs
of Nellie's appearance, and the widow was still standing in the morning-room fidgeting with her gloves.

Nellie was not to be seen anywhere; for so soon
as Lady Frankwell found that the bride-elect did
not come on being called, she sent her own maid,
Percome, and Nellie's, to hunt.

Of course it was a case of *non est inventa.*

Now, Lady Frankwell's head was not an empty
one, as ladies' heads go, yet it was by no means
full enough to make her to see through this new
millstone that had suddenly started up. She was
not flurried as Mrs. Branston, but she was puzzled.
She gave herself up to thought for a while, being

interrupted in the midst of her deliberations by the old housekeeper.

"Well, Davis," began her ladyship.

"I've just come to tell you, my lady, something that has just struck me, and I thought it best to mention it, because it's rather strange, and may have something to do with nobody being able to find Miss Branston in the house. You remember that gentleman that used to be at the rectory, my lady, that gentleman who was Mr. Branston's pupil some time ago?"

"Do you mean Lord Richard Grant?"

"No, my lady, no, that wasn't the name; it was a Mr. Somebody; a tall, handsome young gentleman, who had two big dogs and—"

"Mr. Lorford, do you mean?"

"Yes, yes, my lady, Mr. Lorford, that's the name. I'm nearly sure I saw him in the square yesterday. I was out in the afternoon about three o'clock with Kerwood, and came across a gentleman whose face I knew at once, but I could not think of his name do all I would. He was looking up at this house rather hard, I thought; but I didn't think anything of that at the time, and I supposed he was going to call. I forgot all about him till supper, when Kerwood told me she had seen the same gentleman in the square, looking up at the house as he was before. I asked Biggs if he had called. Biggs remembered the gentleman at once when I described him, my lady, and he said he had not been here. If you remember, my lady, he was very fond of Miss Branston; and the servants used to say that they thought he meant something, and the lady's maid at the rectory said she thought Miss Branston liked Mr. Lorford, because——"

" Stay a minute, Davis. You are quite sure it was Mr. Lorford you saw ?"

" Positive, my lady, certain ; and Kerwood is sure it was the same gentleman she saw the second time in the evening."

" There is something strange in this, as you say, and I hardly know what to think. If Miss Branston were in the house she would have been found ; and it is not likely she would be anywhere but in her own room, or the drawing-room, or one of the two rooms down here. If she has left the house, and it seems almost absurd that she should leave it, she must have gone out by the breakfast-room window. I'll go and see if it is open."

And her ladyship went, and found the window, and likewise the door leading into the mews open.

" I believe she must have gone, my lady, and gone too with Mr. Lorford."

Lady Frankwell reflected.

The idea of an elopement had struck her, but she could hardly bring herself to believe such an improbability possible.

She had so few grounds to go upon. That Mr. Lorford was in town she did not doubt, but she was as positive as she could be that he and Nellie had not met, and that no letter had passed between them.

She asked Biggs and the footmen if they had taken any letters to Miss Branston. No.

Her ladyship then went to the widow, and as she crossed the hall, a sudden thought came into her mind to the effect that she might have been completely misled as to the extent of Nellie's regard for Mr. Lorford. Nellie might have been desperately in love with him, and her mother might have concealed this fact when she saw there was a chance of marrying her to Sir Harry.

Lady Frankwell went straight to the point, and plumply said to the widow, "It's my belief, Mrs. Branston, that Fenella has eloped."

"Eloped, Lady Frankwell! eloped? With whom, with whom? Oh! no, no! impossible. She must be somewhere; do let the servants search the whole house."

" Quite enough search has been made, Mrs. Branston ; Fenella is not *in* the house, I feel sure. The question is, with whom has she left it? *I* believe with Mr. Lorford ; yes, with Mr. Lorford ; he has twice been seen in the square, and—— "

"Impossible, impossible, Lady Frankwell."

" It is my belief that Fenella's affections were pre-engaged to a far greater extent than I had any idea of. It is by no means impossible that Mr. Lorford may have been in London for some time, and that, by some means, he may have got a letter into Fenella's hands without our seeing it : through a letter he could easily arrange time and place for an escape. I cannot, however, pretend to tell *how* the elopement has been accomplished, but of the fact I think there is very little doubt. If Fenella ever loved Mr. Lorford at all, of which I now feel only too certain, she loved him well enough to elope with him, and my son's attentions must have been like so much poison to the poor girl. Harry has been deceived through me, and I—— "

Her ladyship had the words " through you " on the tip of her tongue, but she jerked them back into her mouth, and swept out of the room.

The widow's intellect was far too dense to take in more than the faintest outlines of Lady Frankwell's

speech : she sat upon the sofa in a complete fog of
bewilderment.

Lady Frankwell ran up to her *boudoir.* Taking
a sheet of note-paper she wrote hastily thereupon,

" *Come back at once, my dear Harry. Fenella
is nowhere to be found. I believe she has eloped.*"

F. F.

" Biggs, take this at once to the coachman, and
bid him hurry off directly to Allhallows. John must
go with the carriage to deliver the note in the
Church to the sacristan, the man in the black gown,
who must be told to hand it, as quietly as possible,
to Sir Harry."

Sir Harry and Lord Huntingsdale had been for
some time awaiting Nellie's arrival in the Chancel,
and the rest of the bridal party were beginning to
share their impatience.

The congregation too, numbering over seven
hundred, seemed very tired of the squashing and
crushing, and longed for the event of the day, the
arrival of the bride-elect, to distract their attention.

But very little time elapsed before Sir Harry received his mother's message.

" By Jove, she's bolted, Hunty," he said ; forgetting where he was, and speaking above a whisper.

The expression of his face at once proclaimed to
the lookers-on that something had gone wrong, and
the idea was confirmed when he hurriedly left the
Church, and Lord Huntingsdale went into the
vestry.

This was very sad for the eight parsons, for the
squashed congregation, and the three organ-blowers !

There were, at fewest, two hundred young ladies
of the congregation perfectly willing to step up to
the Altar, and do duty for the absent one. Not one

could understand why a girl should fail to appear
when such a good looking fellow as Sir Harry was
waiting to change her name.

Yet how delightfully romantic! how charming to
be able to say at Lady Downfal's next assembly,
"*I* was at Allhallows the day that Sir Harry
Frankwell was *not* married!"

The Church rapidly began to get very roomy,
whilst the disconcerted organ-blowers, especially
the third man, sank into their very thick boots.

Harry hardly knew what to think or make of the
matter. He got into the carriage smiling; before
he had gone fifty yards he put his head out of the
window and shouted, "Richards, if you don't make
those horses go faster, I'll get out of the carriage
and drive myself."

Then he leaned back, tearing his gloves off, and
then he tried to stand upright.

Arrived at number 53, he darted out of the carriage into the hall, amidst a crowd of staring idlers
that lined the entrance.

"Where's her ladyship, Biggs?"

"In the *boudoir*, Sir Harry."

Up there he darted, and found his mother in
tears.

"My dearest Harry——"

"My dearest mother, don't cry, it's all right,
never mind me, don't cry, *I*'ve not eloped!"

He was a queer fellow, my reader, but we must
believe that he only took this queer view of the
question in order to soothe his good mother.

"I only hope she's not been abduced—abducted,
what do you call it, abducted by some infernal
scoundrel; by Jove, I'll kill him."

" No, Harry, I believe she has gone off with some one she—she I—loves."

" With some one she loves? what, does she love half a dozen fellows? She's not gone off with me, that's certain, and I was always under the impression that she loved *me*."

" With somebody she loved years ago."

" What, an old attachment? Why the devil did nobody tell me of this? I thought she never loved any fellow but me; why the deuce was I not told all? Good gracious me, does anybody think that I can't find a lovable girl in this world to have me, without my having to cut some fellow out? Why, I'd as soon think of cutting a fellow out, as —mother, dearest, don't cry. If Nellie has eloped with somebody she loves, she's all right. I care for her a great deal more than I care for myself. If she'll be happier with this other fellow than with me, why, I'm the last fellow in the world to regret what she has done. But I did love her, by Jove, I did, and — oh! don't cry, dearest mother, don't cry."

He kissed his mother a dozen times, and stayed her tears after a while.

Then, hearing a great noise of chattering amongst the servants in the hall, and also amongst the crowd outside, he shouted from the top of the stairs, " Can't some of you fools down there shut the door, or do you mean those dirty beggars outside to come in and eat the breakfast? Biggs, bring me a bottle of champagne, and look sharp. Mother dearest, I must fortify myself: losing Nellie is no joke, but I hope she'll be happy; by Jove, I hope she loves this other fellow like mad, and that he loves her as much. But what's his name, do you know?"

"Well, Harry, dear, I believe, but of course I cannot speak with certainty, that Mr. Lorford, who used to be at the rectory as a pupil, is——."

"The happy man. Archibald Brudenel Lorford, I remember the name quite well, but I always missed seeing him, confound it. Well, mother, dear, he's a lucky fellow: stolen kisses are sweetest, they say, so I expect are stolen brides."

As the butler was passing through the hall, after taking Sir Harry his champagne, Mrs. Branston timidly called him into the morning-room, and timidly said to him, "Biggs, don't you think we had better send for a policeman?"

CHAPTER V.

ON DANGEROUS GROUND.

WHETHER Nellie shelved her conscience in order that she might throw herself into Archibald Lorford's arms, or whether she suddenly lost it, it is impossible to say. The conscience returned to her ere she had gone a hundred yards in the cab, and of course it asked if she were prepared to take the consequences of this desperate step.

Nellie was perfectly ready to undergo anything provided she could have her co-eloper by her side. She could hardly persuade herself that she had positively eloped. She had read of the one great *dernier ressort* which love provides for the desperate, and been immensely interested in the doings of the run-away couples, but to be an actual elopress herself, that was something more than she could contemplate composedly.

" Now, Nellie, darling," said Archibald to her, after the excitement of the sudden flight had somewhat cooled down, " nobody in this world shall separate us ; indeed the question is, rather, who shall join us. We will go to a quiet little village in Staffordshire or Shropshire and be married by special licence to-morrow ; then we will start off for the Isle of Man, and enjoy our honeymoon in peace and seclusion."

Nellie's conscience did not reproach her for having run away, though when she began to reflect that poor Sir Harry might be broken-hearted, her womanly nature excited all her tenderness, and almost set tears a-flowing.

When the question of happiness with Archibald Lorford and of misery with Sir Harry came really to the point, then, as we have seen, Nellie put forth all her strength and let her heart, not her mother, make choice. In one second she overturned the iron altar of Family Advantage : in one second she upset the priest, and not all the king's horses nor all the king's men could set up altar or priest this side upwards again !

Archibald Lorford bade the cabman stop at his hotel, and having there paid his bill and got his luggage, he and Nellie were driven on to Paddington.

Good fortune favoured them in the matter of a train, and in ten minutes they were on their way northwards, Archibald having taken tickets for Shrewsbury. Happily there was no one in the carriage with them, so the extensive budget of news each had to communicate to the other was neither overheard nor interrupted.

The farther they got from London, the braver and happier Nellie Branston felt. Timid she never was, and odd would it have been had she been timid now, seeing that she had love to cheer her, and Archibald Lorford to protect her, and no match-making mother to torment her.

After the train, which was an express, was fairly on its way, Archibald put his arm round Nellie's waist, where probably Sir Harry would have been insinuating his had matters turned out differently, and she, leaning her head upon his shoulder, in a little while closed her eyes, and during a long account of his serenade, hopes, fears, doubts, and agony, fell fast asleep.

An extraordinary elopress verily !

Poor Nellie ! sleep was a strange sensation to her ; she had had none for twenty-four hours, and little enough any night since Sir Harry proposed.

She awoke in about an hour's time, and soon began to chatter again in her own lively way. Never did her voice sound more sweetly in Archie's ears ; never looked her eyes more vanquishingly bright.

She was indeed a beauty, her face so markedly stamped with glowing intelligence, its expression all animation and vivacity ; her dainty little lips most exquisitely formed ; her fine, fair hair rich in its abundance and luxuriance.

As for him who sat by her side, he was possessed of nearly six feet of as good British solidity as was to be seen anywhere, and his broad, manly, shoulders were surmounted by a good, well-shaped head, and by a pleasant face, frank and intelligent in expression, handsome in every feature. Archibald Lorford was of a dark complexion, his hair nearly black. He had massive, well-kept whiskers, and a fine beard covered and adorned the lower part of his face.

He was well worth eloping with, Nellie thought. I need hardly say that he returned the compliment.

Though Archibald hardly knew how the Frankwells could discover anything beyond the very bare but undeniable fact of the elopement, he thought it best not to go the whole way to Shrewsbury by train, as the telegraph might have been made use of in London to tell some unpleasant tales along the line.

Every important station might have been telegraphed to upon every line in the kingdom for all he could tell, though he thought it hardly likely. However he deemed it best to get out one station short of Shrewsbury, and accordingly he and Nellie left the train at Admaston.

Procuring a cab with some little difficulty, the runaways were driven through Longdon-upon-Tern to within three miles of the pleasant little Salopian village of Hadnal.

On getting out, they turned into a large public-house, and, after half an hour's rest, hired a spring-cart from the landlord, and were driven to their destination, the Saracen's Head Hotel, Hadnal.

Here a welcome awaited the gentleman eloper, for the landlady came out, exclaiming, " Well, I never expected to see you, Mr. Archibald, but I'm very glad you've found time at last to have a look at us : come in, sir."

And in went Nellie and Archie, the former not a little surprised to find her protector evidently well known.

The reason of his being well known was a simple one, and consisted in the fact of the landlady having lived eight or nine years with Lady Arabella Lorford, his mother.

On the lady's death, her maid married the butler —a fashionable weakness with ladies' maids—and her husband had taken a hotel, an equally fashionable failing of butlers.

Of course Mrs. Edwards was under the very natural impression that the pretty young lady with Archibald Lorford was his wife, and addressing her as Mrs. Lorford, she asked her to come upstairs to unshawl herself, and wash hands before tea.

Archibald determined within himself to lose no time in seeking out the spiritual ruler of the parish; and after a preliminary conversation, he asked the landlord, who had just come in, where the rector, vicar, or incumbent might live.

On finding the distance to be very short, Archibald resolved to pay him a visit before the severe tea which he had ordered was ready.

Now, an eloper is one who ought to be prepared for anything and everything, who ought to have his sword ever girt upon his thigh; who should never be wanting in any emergency; a man who should bristle with foresight, forethought, and penetration.

Yet it is very hard to have to wear armour perpetually, to be constantly on guard, to be always emergency-sharp. Archibald Lorford was a fair specimen of the genus, and he was pretty well prepared for whatever might happen; but, as we shall find before we come to the end of this chapter, he had a vulnerable part about him; he had one soft, penetrable place in his armour.

He failed in precaution.

He went straight off to the parson without making a single inquiry about him, without even asking his name.

It took our friend some time to work the incumbent round, as the reverend gentleman had a good many questions to ask.

Marrying elopers may be very profitable work, but there are some divines who are rather squeamish on the subject, and none more so, it appeared, than the worthy gentleman Archibald Lorford had fixed upon.

But he did come round in three quarters of an hour, and promised to tie the knot at a quarter to nine o'clock on the following morning.

"And now I must ask your name, if you please."

"Archibald Brudenel Lorford."

"Thank you; related to the Castle Lorford family, I suppose?"

"Yes, I'm a miserable first cousin; a respectable outcast uncomfortably well-born."

"And the young lady's name?"

"Fenella Millicent Branston."

"WHAT? I beg your pardon; what name?"

Archibald repeated it.

Then there was a pause.

"I— I— am afraid, Mr. Lorford, that I shall not— not be——"

"Not be what, sir? Has the young lady's name discomposed you?"

"Not at all, not at all. I am really afraid, however, that I shall not find it convenient to marry you and Miss— Miss Bran— Miss Branston so early as a quarter to nine. I should esteem it a great favour if you would allow me to say eleven o'clock."

"I thought you were going to say you could not marry us at all, sir. Well, really, eleven o'clock would not do, because I want to catch a train in Shrewsbury not far from that time. Might I suggest half-past nine, or ten at the very latest?"

"Well, say ten, Mr. Lorford; I really could not manage it before ten."

"Thank you, thank you. Is the name of Branston familiar to you?"

"Not familiar, certainly; but I have met with it once or twice. It is not actually an uncommon name, and I daresay there are a good many Branstons in most parts of the kingdom."

As if "sagacious of his quarry," Archibald watched the reverend gentleman with the eye of a hawk as he replied to the last question, and when he had finished, bade him good night.

Archibald walked back to the Saracen's Head, whistling "The Young Man from the Country," and altogether looking as happy as a man ought to look who supposed that he was going to be married to-morrow to such a girl as Nellie.

Five minutes after Archibald left the parsonage, the worthy parson clapped a low-crowned hat upon his head, hurried off to the station, and, before long, had arrived in Shrewsbury.

He at once betook himself to the telegraph office, which is most conveniently placed as far as possible from every other office, and immediately wrote out a message.

He wrote out three, if not more, before he was satisfied with his handiwork; and all the time of writing, did not look as if he altogether liked the job.

The reverend gentleman was very nervous, and would have given a great deal to have been spared his present undertaking. His message might cause much mischief, and he went so far as to fear that blood might flow from it. Love and duty, however, combined, gave him nerve enough to determine to telegraph, let the consequences be what they might.

He was half afraid he had cut his own throat by his unguarded, impulsive conduct before Archibald

Lorford. His want of tact, or display of surprise on hearing Nellie's name, might have suggested to Archibald's keen nose the presence of a rat, and if so, the object of the telegraphing might be frustrated.

Telegraph however he would, and telegraph he did, thus :—

"J. H. Frankwell, Hadnal, to Sir H. K. Frankwell, Bart., 53, Cavendish Square, London, W

"*Miss Branston is here with a Mr. Archibald Lorford. I have been asked to marry them to-morrow. Telegraph back instantly. I shall wait at Shrewsbury station for answer.*"

Telling the clerk he would call again in about an hour's time for the chance of getting an answer, the Reverend James Harvey Frankwell—for such was his name—lit a cigar, and ruminated as he smoked. "I hope Harry will come down with the mail and take the affair out of my hands altogether. But I must see him first. I must have no fighting. Poor Harry! he used to write so enthusiastically about this Miss Branston; such an impulsive fellow, so devoted, will be half a lunatic on finding that he has lost her. However, the telegraph may be able to save him."

It would certainly have been as well for Archibald Lorford to have asked the parson's name before calling upon him, inasmuch as the reverend gentleman was a Frankwell, an appellation by no means harmonious in sound to the eloper's ears at the present time. He was, in fact, a first cousin of Sir Harry, and had been asked to perform the marriage ceremony at Allhallows.

Why he was prevented it matters not.

When he had finished his cigar, the Reverend James returned to the telegraph office, and anxiously asked if a message had been received.

None had as yet arrived, but there came one in a few minutes' time, and we will, for the present, leave the incumbent to spell it over carefully.

It was a message which he could hardly understand at first.

Those of my worthy readers, whether they be of elopement calibre or not, who look upon themselves as amazingly acute judges of human nature, and of man's capabilities, must pause ere they censure Archibald Lorford for want of foresight or for carelessness. You cannot exactly say of an eloper, *nascitur non fit*, though of course his conduct in emergencies has much to do with the spirit, character, and temperament with which he may have been endowed by nature.

At all events, experience alone can teach a man the entirely correct thing in elopements!

CHAPTER VI.

FACE TO FACE.

"IT is not *I* who have eloped, my dear mother, do bear that in mind. I am not going to leave you, and bolt with some Miss Lorford. As for that diabolical old widow, if she does not clear out of the house in two hours, I'll take my foot to her; yes, by Jove, I'll kick her out."

"No, no, Harry dear, she's a woman."

"Yes, mother, she *is* a woman, she's not a giraffe; such a creature as that could be nothing but a woman. She is the mother of Nellie though, and that's enough to make her a C.B. By Jove, the society of Nellie has reformed me; it has set me up in a moral point of view. I've lost a good example, it is true, but she has left good seeds behind her. She was so quiet, gentle and ladylike, and I thought it was not her way to be demonstrative to me. It never struck me that she did not love me, or of course I'd have dropped the love-making like a hot potato. I must do something now, or go somewhere, though I can never forget Nellie; no, not if I take lodgings on Tristan d'Acunha, wherever that may be. But I'll carry out the reform I have begun. I'll turn over a new leaf, and at once give Limmins a good hiding for trying to set me against my brother Gil."

"My dear Harry, pray don't turn over your new leaf with your fists; do leave Mr. Limmins alone,

and see a little less of him than you used. I trust,
my dear boy, you will soon get over this terrible
shock."

"A great deal sooner than Limmins would get
over his shock if I hammered him as he deserves.
Bless you, mother, I've half got over the shock already. I shall be next door to happy directly the
widow clears out, and I must have her out this
very day. I'll go and tell her now, that she'll have
to shuffle off this Cavendish Square coil before
night."

And off Sir Harry went to the morning-room,
where he found the widow weeping. He fully meant
to be savage, but he would have been no man had
he long retained this savagery after finding the
weaker vessel in tears.

"Hollo, Mrs. Branston, are you laying the dust
as well as my mother? Come, don't cry; it's all
right, you know. Nellie is all right, and she is the
chief person to be considered. I'd have done just
the same thing myself, for nobody can expect a
girl to marry Jones when she loves Smith."

The widow hardly knew what to expect when
she saw Sir Harry come into the room.

Did he guess that Archibald Lorford was the one
who had run off with the bride-elect? Did he
know anything of Archibald's love for Nellie?
Did he know that she, the widow, had lyingly
stated that this love had long since vanished?

Sir Harry's manner, however, put her comparatively at ease: he had not come, apparently, to eat
or slaughter her; he had not come, it seemed, to
hand her over to Sir Richard Mayne & Co. Yes,
his natural, off-hand way of talking, made her think
that nothing very dreadful was going to happen.

She had not the least idea what on earth to say
to him.

She managed to begin thus, however :

" I am very sorry indeed, Sir Harry, for what
has happened ; but— but——"

" Of course you are sorry, but I am not. Now,
why the deuce did you not tell me weeks ago about
this Mr. Lorford, of whom my mother has been
speaking to me ?   Why wouldn't you let the poor
girl be happy ?"

" Because, Sir Harry, because I thought Mr.
Lorford a drunken dissipated man."

" Now you thought nothing of the sort."

" Indeed, Sir Harry, I did ; indeed I did.   I saw
him stagger once."

" Stagger be hung.   Even supposing you did
think him a loose fish, you know as well as my
mother knows, that there is hardly a looser fish in
the kingdom than myself, and yet you would willingly give your daughter to me.   Now, there's a
nasty thorn in your conscience, you know, and
you'd better take it out.   You misled my mother
in the matter of Nellie's affections ; now didn't
you ?"

Widow *tacet.*

" Of course, you did," continued Sir Harry, " because you thought that I was better game than Mr.
Lorford ; the idea of loose fishiness being quite a
secondary consideration.   I am better than he certainly as game, though for family, birth, and that
sort of thing, Lorfords are as good as Frankwells
all over the world.   Now, don't you think you've
acted very cruelly towards your daughter, and can
you, for a moment, be surprised at what you have
driven her to ?   I thank Nellie for running off from
me.   I would have worshipped at her feet all my

F

life, such was my love for her ; but if she gave me
no real love in return, I had rather have died at her
feet before the Altar than have married her."

As Sir Harry said this, he appeared to be not a
little moved himself, and his handkerchief more
than once found its way to his eyes.

" Now, be honest, Mrs. Branston, and pull that
nasty thorn out of your conscience : you did mislead my mother, and all because you wanted Nellie
to make what folks call a good match.   Is not that
a fact ?"

Widow *tacebat.*

" Come, I'm pretty honest with you, I think,"
said Sir Harry.

" I will leave you to-day, Sir Harry, and I shall
consider it my duty to repay you all——"

" Now, you'll neither leave nor repay me anything.   You will just be honest.   There's nothing
like giving your conscience a periodical clearing out,
and you'll not feel happy till you have got rid of a
deal of old lumber.   Come, Mrs. Branston, be
honest."

Then the widow, in the midst of a fresh burst of
tears, sobbed forth—" Forgive me, Sir Harry, forgive me !   I—I——"

" Of course I forgive you ; it's all right now.
You did know that Nellie loved Mr. Lorford, and
very deeply too ?"

" I did."

" And you did mislead my mother ?"

" Yes, Sir Harry."

" Now, I'm not going to ask or say any more.
Come, dry your eyes and take my arm, we'll go to
my mother and tell her it is all right.   I've forgiven
you, I've forgiven you, and you'll hear no more of
this, Mrs. Branston.   Scheming mothers are as

thick as weeds all over the kingdom, and much as I hate them, I make allowances for them, because they are human nature from top to toe. Come along."

The widow, however, felt quite unable to move, and was overwhelmed in what literally seemed a flood of tears.

"Now, there's nothing to fear from any one, my good woman; dry your tears. If any one ought to be crying, I am the one, I think. Now, if you don't dry up at once, I'll—I'll set fire to you!"

At which idea Mrs. Branston could not help a very homœopathic smile, which broke the rush of tears, and in a minute or two she accompanied Sir Harry to Lady Frankwell's boudoir.

In five minutes Sir Harry had arranged everything beautifully between the widows, and much ashamed though Mrs. Branston felt, still Lady Frankwell's kind manner and Sir Harry's honest, off-hand good nature went far to smother the shame, though, at the same time, it heightened her sorrow for what she had done.

When she had gone upstairs to put herself a little bit straight for luncheon, Lady Frankwell threw her arms round her son's neck, and kissing him, said—"You're a good fellow, Harry, my boy, you are indeed."

"Not a bit, not a bit; I'm natural, that's all. It knocks me down to see a woman unhappy: besides, Mrs. Branston is not one screw worse than one million mothers in England. As for that Mr. Lorford, if he's a perfect Satan now, which I don't believe he is, Nellie will make a St. Paul of him in a month, for I suppose we may conclude that he is the gentleman who has walked off with my promised bride. Dash it, mother, I used to think girls were all crinoline, shoulders, and back-hair; but hang me, if they don't carry more Heaven about with them than anything else."

" Well, dear Harry," said Lady Frankwell, after a short pause, " a good deal of the blame connected with this matter ought to fall upon my shoulders. I was always bothering you to get married, and I hustled you into falling in love with Fenella. I saw a girl whom I considered suitable, one who seemed to me in every way desirable for a good-natured, wild fellow like you, and I was not happy until I heard that you had proposed to her. I'm just as bad a woman as poor Mrs. Branston."

" Nonsense, dear mother, nonsense: I'll set fire to you, if you hold such preposterous ideas. I fell in love with Nellie of my own accord, and I take uncommon credit for my good taste. Holloa! there's Huntingsdale crossing the square, and evidently making for 53. I must go down and speak to him."

No one who saw Sir Harry at luncheon that day would have supposed that only two hours previously he had lost what he considered the prettiest and most lovable girl in the world. Lord Huntingsdale even, who well knew his high-spiritedness and mercurial temperament, was vastly surprised.

After luncheon the two widows took a drive, to freshen themselves up, and to enjoy a little quiet discussion.

Mrs. Branston was very penitent, and, carried away by the pleasure of emptying her conscience of what Sir Harry had called ' old lumber,' made herself out to be far worse than she really was.

Sir Harry went out for a drive in his brougham with Lord Huntingsdale, and the two consulted as to what ought to be done for the best in the matter

of the supposed elopement. They could come to
no conclusion whatever: Sir Harry's only thought
was for Nellie's protection; if she had gone off
with Archibald Lorford she was all right.

But suppose some vagabond had entrapped her
and carried her off?

That was highly improbable, they both agreed.
Their final resolve was to take no action till the
morning, a delay, Sir Harry thought, by no means
dangerously long, so convinced was he that Nellie
had gone off with Mr. Lorford.

An hour or two after dinner, on Sir Harry's return
to the drawing-room, after a post-prandial cigar, a
violent knocking was heard at the front door, and
an equally vigorous pulling of the bell.

The widow started.

She fully expected to see Nellie dragged into the
room by a policeman !

She was much relieved when the butler came in
with a telegraphic message for Sir Harry.

"By Jove, mother, never met with such an extraordinary thing in my life: it's like a novel: I know
what I'll do."

"Harry, Harry, may I see the message ?" cried
Lady Frankwell, as her son rushed to the door.

"No, dear mother, not now: it is only of importance to me. I shall see you again to-morrow;
good-night: nothing horrible; on the contrary,
good news for us all. Nellie is safe and as comfortable as a sugar-loaf."

And Sir Harry hurried out of the room, leaving
the two widows not a little perplexed.

———

Nellie had washed her hands and returned into
the private sitting-room of the Saracen's Head

some little while before Archibald Lorford came
back from the parsonage.

She looked all the better for having smartened
herself up a bit, and Archibald felt immensely
proud of his bride-elect.

After two or three of those kisses, whose intensity is known only to elopers, Archibald gave Nellie
an account of his interview with the reverend
gentleman, and he gave her also to understand that
matters had not gone quite so comfortably as he
would have wished.

"By some extraordinary piece of ill-luck, dear
Nellie, I believe we have fled into the enemy's
country. Let us see: one question and its answer
will probably settle all."

When the tea was finished, the servant came
to 'clear away,' and then Archibald said to her,
"Martha, Matilda, Mary, Margaret, Susan, Jemima,
Jane, what is the name of the clergyman
here ? "

" Mr. Frankwell, sir."

Then did Nellie start.

After the servant had gone, Archibald said, " I
thought there was something in the wind, Nellie
dear : the parson was no diplomatist : I saw half
way through him while talking to him, and Jemima
Jane has enabled me to see through the other
half."

" Well, Archie, I suppose we must leave Hadnal
before the time fixed for the wedding, and put it
out of the power of Mr. Frankwell to molest us in
any way."

"Yes, my sensible Nellie, we will leave here
early to-morrow morning so as to be in Shrewsbury
to catch the 7.38 for Chester, and by this means
we shall frustrate any charitable exertions the

reverend gentleman may see fit to make on behalf
of his namesake."

"But he may have made some already, Archie,
and——"

"He has not had time to do anything this
evening, Nellie, dear."

So Archibald thought.

We have seen, however, that the reverend gentleman was particularly sharp and smart. Colin
Campbellism was as much his characteristic as it
was the widow's.

Archibald Lorford had not a little difficulty in
persuading Mrs. Edwards that Nellie was not his
lawfully wedded wife; so much difficulty indeed
that he had to confess the elopement.

To a sober-minded, propriety-tight woman like
the good landlady, this was a confession of a start-
ling and astounding nature.

The confession, however, led her to prepare a
comfortable little room for Nellie's nocturnal
reception, and thereto the bride-elect presently
betook herself, with a rather unpleasant reminder
from Archibald that breakfast would be ready
exactly at six.

Archie himself had a couple of cigars with the
landlord, and then retired for the night to a
chamber usually occupied by successive commer-
cial 'gentlemen.'

The Reverend James Henry Frankwell returned
that night to the parsonage, and he came back
with a message from Sir Harry which greatly
astonished him.

Right well was he aware that of all men in this
world his cousin was pre-eminently the most high-
spirited.

High-spiritedness was essentially the most marked

characteristic of Sir Harry Frankwell; nothing seemed able to subdue him; he was never beaten by anything; he never yet felt down or done.

He was also one of the best-natured fellows alive, as the incumbent well knew. Though for a day or two he believed what his umbrageous friend Limmins had told him about his brother Gilbert, he did not for a second change his affection towards his brother, nor did he allow the scandalous charge to remain an hour in his mind. But he certainly hoped to check any longing there might be for baronetcy or property by taking unto himself a wife, a strange proceeding, followed occasionally by one which the world looks upon as a little stranger. Sir Harry's good spirits alone had served to keep him from realizing the loss he had sustained in being deprived of the life-companionship of Nellie. It was all right, he thought; it was the most sensible thing she could do to elope with the man she loved, far more sensible than to go tamely to the Altar with a man she did not love.

The substance and spirit of this the Reverend James Henry Frankwell read in the message he had just received.

"Poor Harry!" he said to himself, "if he's a queer, madcap fellow, he's a good-hearted one, and most surely he deserves not to be a victim of woman's inconstancy. I shall do nothing about this elopement till morning. O woman! woman! woman!"

And do I then wonder that Julia deceives me,
 When surely there's nothing in nature more common?
She vows to be true and while vowing she leaves me,
 But could I expect any more from a woman?

O woman! your heart is a pitiful treasure;
  And Mahomet's doctrine was not too severe,
When he thought you were only materials of pleasure,
  And reason and thinking were out of your sphere!

By your heart, when the fond sighing lover can win it,
  He thinks then an age of anxiety's paid;
But oh! while he's blest, let him die on the minute—
  If he lives but a *day*, he'll be surely betray'd!
                                        Moore.

With these lines in his mind our reverend friend, who himself had once suffered from an affair of the heart, lay down to rest soon after his return home.

She, whom he so cruelly maligned, for he believed fair Nellie inconstancy itself, enjoyed such rest as she had not known since the day poor Sir Harry proposed, and it was not without a struggle that she divorced herself at 5.30 A.M. from Mrs. Edwards' comfortable sheets. But elopers cannot expect everything to go smoothly; they must take the bitter with the sweet. You cannot see a smart burlesque without having to undergo a senseless break-down.

At half-past six the Saracen's Head cab was at the door, and in two minutes more the run-away couple were on their way to Shrewsbury. When they reached the station the porters were occupied in attending to the wants of passengers about to start by a train bound for the direction of Hadnal; so Archibald, finding that he could get no assistance with his luggage in any direction whatever, and, moreover, that his own train would not start for twenty minutes, bethought him that a cup of coffee would do Nellie no harm. He accordingly took her to the refreshment room and there left her.

Just at this moment a young gentleman, wearing

a fashionable, light overcoat, rushed into the station, and commenced looking everywhere for somebody to carry a portmanteau and large travelling case for him.

No porter appeared, and he was just going to shoulder the portmanteau himself, when Archibald Lorford, who had been watching him, came up and volunteered his assistance.

"Let me help you, sir, let me help you; porters and policemen are much of a kind in an emergency."

"Thank you, by Jove, you're a brick. I'm awfully obliged to you. It is a lady's portmanteau and so deuced heavy that I should fancy she must be in the habit of wearing steel armour instead of dresses."

With our eloping friend's assistance, portmanteau and travelling case were soon carried to the opposite platform.

Then Archibald came back to look after Nellie, accompaied by the young gentleman whom he had been helping.

The two were laughing very merrily as they crossed the bridge.

"I'll tell you what, I wish you'd help me to put a bottle of champagne out of sight," said Archie's new friend. "It is rather early to indulge the *cacoëthes bibendi* certainly, but Shropshire champagne is very harmless, I daresay. I suppose they have some here that passes for the real Clicquot article amongst Shrewsbury gooseberry drinkers. Come into the refreshment room; don't you say ' No' if you had rather not."

And in Archie went with his new friend, resolved, however, to partake but sparingly of the sparkling fluid.

Nellie was sitting at one of the little side tables, putting on her gloves, and feeling all the better for the coffee.

Her co-eloper's new friend was walking up to the counter, which, however, was so stuffed up by the hungry and thirsty that he could not get within two or three yards of it.

Casting his eyes over the travellers in the room he re-commenced talking to Archie; suddenly he started, and rushed to the table whereat pretty Nellie was sitting.

" By Jove !"

And Nellie was face to face with—Sir Harry Frankwell.

CHAPTER VII.

SIR HARRY AND THE ELOPERS.

SIR HARRY, on reading his cousin's telegram, made up his mind in one second how to act. He rushed out of the drawing-room and ordered a cab to be fetched immediately, and in about three minutes' time was on his way to Paddington.

Arrived at the station, he at once telegraphed to the Reverend James Henry as follows :

> "*Marry them by all means : it's all right : a case of elopement : old attachment. Stop, don't marry them unless the man be a big, dark, strong, muscular, handsome fellow : isn't she pretty ? I'm all right : soon get over it. Don't take any fee.*"

This message the incumbent of Hadnal read with less ease than have you, most excellent reader, inasmuch as electricity does not mind its stops.

He was puzzled ; but it was clear that the elopers were to be wedded, so he had nought to do but wed them.

He took the message home, determined to cancel what his cautiousness had dictated, by getting up early and sending an intimation to Mr. Lorford that the wedding could most conveniently be celebrated at 8.45. But he did not get up early enough for Archibald Lorford, and his note was brought back by the landlord ten minutes after it was sent, with the unexpected intelligence that Mr.

Lorford had left the village exactly half an hour ago.

Sir Harry having telegraphed, took it into his sadly empty head to run down to Shrewsbury and startle the elopers, if possible, after the wedding. But on the suggestion of this not so sadly empty head, he determined to make his journey one of use. So he got into a Hansom, drove back full tilt to Cavendish Square, sent for a four-wheeler; had Nellie's luggage put therein, drove off again to Paddington, and just caught the last train that would take him to Shrewsbury.

He put up at the Raven Hotel; got up early, feeling restless, and took his ticket, with Nellie's luggage for Hadnal.

At the station he met the elopers, as we are aware.

"By Jove!" he exclaimed, as he stood before Nellie and shook her by the hand, "only fancy, I have run the fox to earth. Where are the police? Where are the police? Now don't be frightened, Nellie, Miss Branston, or Mrs. Lorford I mean; I am the best friend you have upon earth, and have no wish to do anything unkind. Where is Mr. Lorford? *I* want to see if he is the right one; if he is, I'll shake hands with him: if he isn't, that is, if he is a scamp and if you have been run off with against your will, I'll kill him."

At this moment Archibald Lorford came up to Nellie, not a little surprised to find that the young gentleman he had assisted was apparently well known to his bride-elect.

"This is Mr. Lorford, Sir Harry," said Nellie, in a low, gentle voice, which plainly betokened her nervousness.

"Then how are you, Mr. Lorford? how are

you ? We were very near neighbours years ago,
at least my home was uncommonly near your temporary one, but, to my knowledge, we never met.
My name is Frankwell, Harry Frankwell, and I've
come down here to bring Nellie— Miss Br—
Mrs. Lorford's luggage. By Jove, Nellie, you had
to sleep in your fawn-coloured silk last night !"

Archibald hardly knew what to say to the man
from whom he had stolen the beautiful girl beside
him.

Sir Harry saw his pausing confusion.

" It's all right, Mr. Lorford, it's all right, you
know ; don't think about me, I'm all right; it was
a mistake altogether. I know what you are thinking
about. I had no more idea that Nell— that this old
friend of mine, whatever be her name now, loved
anybody when I fell in love with her than—than
that fly on the cloth ; by Jove, I've caught it ! but
we heard it yesterday, so it's all right now. It's
only just and right that you should have her as
she loves you. I really mean what I say, for I
invariably say what I think. I'm an awful fellow
for speaking out, and being what I call natural."

Nellie, while she felt assured by Sir Harry's
manner, nevertheless could not avoid feeling very
far from comfortable. She could not help thinking
of what the man, from whom she had run away,
had done, on the most liberal scale, for her mother,
herself, and her brothers. The very things she
wore were his gift; the handsome dress and bracelets his own choosing. This was a secondary
consideration, one of no concern compared with the
fact of the elopement. But Nellie's mind wandered
to Sir Harry's numerous presents, to his great
kindnesses to her family, rather than to the elopement. The latter was an act of self-defence, an

act which it was impossible to avoid committing,
seeing the greatness of the temptation put before
her; an act which Sir Harry himself had just now
justified, when, in his off-hand way, he had said
that of course Archie ought to have her, as she
loved him.

Nellie's mind was singularly easy as to the running away; she treated the matter in a way that
seemed philosophical to her; but no female philo-
sophy that she possessed could bring an atom of
comfort when she thought of all Sir Harry had
given to her and hers, from the fawn-coloured silk
upwards and downwards.

And Archibald Lorford thought this meeting
was fraught with a great deal of embarrassment
which Sir Harry, by his novel mode of reasoning,
had in some way increased and in some way
lessened.

Had it been necessary to receive Sir Harry with
fists, then with fists Archibald would have found
no difficulty in receiving him; but Sir Harry had
offered his open hand, and instead of doing what
used to be customary when the elopers were caught
by the irate parent or the would-be benedict, had
said that it was 'all right!'

He could plainly see that Sir Harry was a
straightforward fellow; that he was a queer fish
certainly, and an honest fish, and that he was not
rattling on in this way to occupy time and attention whilst preparations of a prehensile nature were
going on behind the scenes.

Archibald had little time for reflecting, however,
for Sir Harry's pauses were very short ones.

"And are you married yet? did my cousin
Jemmy at Hadnal read the let-no-man-put-asunder
service? Ah! you look surprised at me knowing

about your going to Hadnal and walking into the
lion's mouth in the shape of the Reverend James.
I must tell you what he did."

And Sir Harry told them ; and when Archibald
said that the wedding had not yet been celebrated,
of course Sir Harry wanted to know the place that
had been fixed upon.

Archibald would not have been surprised had he
offered to give the bride away !

" We thought of being married in Chester, Sir
Harry."

" Capital place ; you can be married there *sub
rosâ*, under the Rows ! ha ! ha ! ha ! Get the
bishop, deans, and half a dozen canons to make
the nuptial knot as much like the Gordian as possible. Where is your train ? I'll help you with
your luggage ; you helped me with mine, you
know. By Jove, we've not had that champagne
yet. Waiter, bring that Shropshire chamgoose-
berrypagne here. You must come and see your
mother, Nell—Miss Branston—when you come
back from your tour. By Jove, what do you think
she wanted to do when she found that the love-bird
had flown ? Send for a policeman ! ha ! ha ! ha !
But you've not told me how you managed matters ;
come, Mr. Lorford, I am a queer fellow, you know,
and should like to hear. I like a fellow that has
the pluck to elope ; I do indeed."

" Well, Sir Harry, you are a queer fellow, I'll
very readily allow ; but I must say it seems unnatural that——"

" Unnatural ! Bless me, I thought I did everything so naturally. What does society do under
similar circumstances ? Would society pitch into
you or send for a peeler ? or set the detectives and
telegraph going ? No, no ; what the deuce would

be the use of behaving otherwise than I am? Nothing in this world I could do would make Miss Branston love me up to marrying point, and what do folks marry for but for love? I'm not such a fool as I look, believe me. The whole thing has been done on the wrong side of the hedge; I don't blame anybody now; I've had a talk, and it's all right. I'm natural; I do things in a natural way; hang it, Mr. Lorford, you cannot deny that. I'm not society; I'm a loose fish, with lots of common sense about me; and, moreover, I'm the last fellow in the world to make an affectionate, tender-hearted girl unhappy."

Archibald Lorford shook Sir Harry very warmly by the hand; and when the two looked at Nellie, they saw that something had touched her tender heart, and that it was relieving itself with tears.

All this had gone on in the refreshment-room; but no one had heard Sir Harry's frank and enthusiastic speech, as our friends were some distance from the counter or bar where the few hungry and thirsty in the room congregated.

"Come, Miss Branston," said Sir Harry, "you have the tenderest heart in the kingdom, but I pray you shed no tears on my account; do not let one thought about me mar the enjoyment of your honeymoon, or of one hour of what I trust will be a long and happy married life. I'm all right, indeed I am. I am your best friend on earth, and I hope your husband will so regard me. I am in a pretty good position, and, by Jove, it will give me real pleasure to employ some of the good things of this world that I possess for the benefit of you and yours. Good bye, good bye."

Then Sir Harry shook hands with Nellie, and was about to take the same leave of Archibald,

G

when the latter said, "No, I can't let you go with
a shake only, Sir Harry. Nellie, dear, stay here
three minutes, I should like to speak——"

"My dear Mr. Lorford, excuse me, you want
probably to speak on subjects to which I won't
listen. It's all right; six words from you can
make me feel unnatural, or wretched, or anything
but what I feel now Please to remember that I
am not society; I like a good shake of the fist;
give it me."

Archibald Lorford held out his hand, and in
another half minute Sir Harry was gone.

"He would have made you a good husband,
Nellie dear;" to which remark Nellie made no reply, but her heart gave most earnest acquiescence.

Sir Harry spent most of the day with his cousin
at Hadnal, returning late in the evening to London.

In due course Archibald Lorford and Nellie
Branston were married, and after a while they
settled in Scotland. There we must leave them,
but not for long, as much has to happen to them,
as likewise to our friend Sir Harry, before time can
have travelled far on his chronic journey.

It is not to be supposed that Sir Harry's exube-
rance of spirits could last for ever. There is, un-
happily, an inevitable combination of feelings and
sensations which tend to produce what is known as
reaction, and to this our high-spirited friend fell a
victim.

On the second day after his return from Shrewsbury, he gave the first symptoms of inevitable depression.

His tongue had a holiday.

Lady Frankwell never remembered him so quiet
in her life, and she fancied she noticed a change in
the tone of his voice. Instead of getting irritable

if he were kept waiting for anything, he became most patient and quiet, often forgetting he had asked for this or that if he did not receive it immediately.

Of course Lady Frankwell tried to enliven him, and the other widow made some disjointed efforts in a similar direction, but all to little purpose.

Lord Huntingsdale, Bob Howard, Limmins, Graham, Menzies, and lots of jolly fellows called, but none entered the house, for Sir Harry was out to everybody.

Sir Harry occupied himself in a very novel study —thinking.

Then he turned to an almost equally novel one to him—reading.

And he read on dreamily, till he came to a passage which seemed to send an electric spark through his brain. He found it in *What will he do with it?*

"He who doth not smoke, hath either known no great griefs, or refuseth himself the softest consolation next to that which comes from heaven. 'What, softer than woman?' whispers the young reader. Young reader, woman teases as well as consoles. Woman makes half the sorrows which she boasts the privilege to soothe. Woman consoles us, it is true, whilst we are young and handsome; when we are old and ugly, woman snubs and scolds us. On the whole, then, woman in this scale, the weed in that, Jupiter, hang out thy balance and weigh them both; and if thou give the preference to woman, all I can say is, the next time Juno ruffles thee, O Jupiter! try the weed!"

"By Jove, I will."

A weed brought Sir Harry some of the consolation held out by the Lord of Knebworth, and the inevitable champagne lent its own peculiar aid.

This prescription Sir Harry followed for two days, and whilst under the influence of the medicine, kept pretty comfortable in mind. But we cannot always be taking medicine. We must allow nature the luxury of enjoying good health sometimes. This Sir Harry soon found out, and so he tried to make the best of himself and of Cavendish Square, without artificial aid.

He went in and out, and usually by himself. Whenever he left the house, however, he felt that he had nothing to look forward to on returning to it, for it was no longer illumined by the happy, bright presence of Nellie. She had quite upset the equilibrium of his general affections, and now she was gone; now her pretty face no longer brought fresh life and spirit in a morning; her sweet voice no longer made sweet music in an evening. Yet it was 'all right,' Sir Harry felt; you cannot expect a girl who loves Smith to marry Jones.

The sight of the widow was not over pleasant, but not a single harsh word did Sir Harry say to her. In a week's time she left, having received an invitation to stay with her only brother in Suffolk, and this departure was a relief and the imparting of a little new life.

About four days after, Lady Frankwell and Sir Harry went down to Hastings, where they were presently joined by Gilbert Frankwell, a lively fellow in the Guards. Here change, excitement, and a good doctor, all of which increasing depression, imperatively demanded, pulled Sir Harry together in about three weeks, and then the old spirits began to revive.

Still he was not quite himself, and this he was not destined to be for some little time, until indeed the happening of one or two events duly to be chronicled.

CHAPTER VIII.

REACTION—DUDSWORTH ELECTION.

TIME passed somewhat pleasantly at Hastings, and our worthy friend, who had grown thin of late, was beginning to find flesh somewhere in the neighbourhood, and gradually managed to transfer it in small quantities to his bones.

Sir Harry was a Jack-in-the-box, who made short work of the lid; it might hold him down for a little while, but somehow or other he would manage to get the better of it, and bob up.

A fruitful source of excitement presented itself about two months after Nellie's marriage, in the resignation of the honourable member for Dudsworth. Sir Harry, not paying much attention to political news at this time, neither saw nor heard anything of the above information, until it was a week old; and it was not for yet two more days that he was aware that a Mr. Rufford Lawson, a gentleman of the Liberal persuasion, had issued an address to the electors of Dudsworth.

"Well, mother, a Liberal never has sat for Dudsworth, and a Liberal never shall while I'm in the world."

"But how are you to avert the calamity, Harry?"

"Why, I'll stand myself; of course I will. I shall be an awful stick at the speaking, like a good many other honourable gentlemen, but I can vote the right way. Give me pen, ink, and paper; I'll write an address like a shot, and in two or three days, Gil and I will bolt to the castle and show ourselves amongst the electors."

It was Sir Harry's nature, we know, to act impulsively, and to carry out, moreover, plans which impulse had led him to form. He wrote out an address in about an hour's time, commencing, "Ladies and gentlemen." Gilbert suggested the omission of the Ladies, and the pen being run through them, the address was complete.

Sir Harry stated his principles very briefly, and wound up by saying, "Of course, you will vote as you like, the tenants on my own property included ; but if you vote for me, you will have the satisfaction of knowing that you are voting for the right man."

This address was posted and sent to the editor of the *Dudsworth Courant,* and a day or two after appeared in that influential publication, and in a separate form on a good many dead walls, in shop windows, and other favourable situations.

Sir Harry's candidature caused surprise to every one, and to no one more than to the honourable Liberal gentleman already in the field, and half way through his canvass.

Sir Harry was sure to be popular ; but still his absence from the castle had cooled down the ardour of many who would otherwise have been his most enthusiastic supporters.

Mr. Lawson lived all but in the borough, and was seldom away from home.

For years he had been doing his best to win the good opinion of the Dudsworthies, giving lectures *gratis,* coming out strong at Penny Readings, taking perpetual chairs, and doing unmistakable charity.

He was now the more popular of the two candidates, but Sir Harry's had ever been the more popular politics.

Sir Harry and his brother Gilbert arrived at Dudsworth Castle, and took counsel with the big Tories of the place..

" When will you commence your canvass, Sir Harry ?"

" Oh, hang the canvass, Mr. Gnokes, I can't do any, really; the electors must consider themselves canvassed."

And nothing would induce Sir Harry to undergo the fatigues and disagreeables of a canvass.

Accompanied by his brother, he showed himself daily in town, drove four-in-hand up to his committee room, made himself agreeable to all voters he met, and altogether went in for the *otium cum dig.* style of candidature.

Of course, he had to do some speaking, though it was long before Mr. Gnokes could induce him to appear in the long room at the Frankwell Arms Hotel to address the worthy electors assembled.

His first attempt was not successful, from a strictly oratorical point of view, but his manner, jolly ways, and thoroughly good style made up for want of eloquence, and he won his way directly.

It was in reply to an inevitable " voice" that he treated his audience to his views on Reform.

" Oh, hang Reform ! the country doesn't want it, and you know that as well as I. Politicians, whether electors or not, must have something to gnaw at, and at the present day they have pitched upon Reform. It's all rubbish, my good friends ; when abuse makes itself evident, then I'll agitate for Reform like a house on fire; but for a wholesale upsetting of the constitution, for a harum-scarum, pell-mell distribution of the franchise, for

an undue preponderance of the democratic element
I'll never vote as long as I've half an ounce of
brains in my head. A revision of the electoral
tariff is perhaps needed, and the suggestions of an
advanced state of civilisation and progress ought
to be carried out, and this will be done, you may be
sure, as readily and heartily by the Tories as
by any men in the kingdom. Mind you, I don't
blame the working men a bit; if they fancy they
have a grievance, being Englishmen, of course
they'll groan and growl. I blame those who so
freely listen to and, as it were, pander to them,
those whose superior education constitutes them
teachers, who therefore ought to tell the unenfranchised working folks that in clamouring for anything below a nine-pound or say an eight-pound
borough franchise, they are howling after a phantom
distinction—after benefits that are all smoke and
vapour."*

A voice, "What about the malt-tax, Sir Harry?"

"Well that is a question upon which I cannot
give an entirely decided opinion; but I tell you
this much, that nothing would give me greater
pleasure than to kick it to the deuce, and the Radi-
cals after it."

On these subjects Sir Harry was badgered a good
deal in the course of the election, but he always
managed to shut up each "voice," not usually with
very satisfactory replies, but with such as provoked
a good deal of laughter, and in that fact he was
contented to think that he had come off best.

There had not been a contested election at Dudsworth for many years, as the place was known to be
almost entirely given to Conservative predilections.

* Spoken some time before the little Bill of 1866 gave up
its little ghost!

Liberals had shown years ago, but nothing more than their faces : now, however, Mr. Rufford Lawson intended to fight it out to the last man, because he felt sure that he had personal popularity to back him.

What sort of a canvass he had had he did not say, in any of his numerous speeches : if cheers, however, were any criterion, he certainly ought to be at the head of the poll, if not a little higher. He buttered the ill-used working men lavishly : told his audiences that Tories were men who did not put on the drag on the coach of Progress as it came *down* hill only, but kept it on during the struggle *up* hill, with many other taking illustrations of the retrogressiveness of Sir Harry's policy, all of which vastly pleased the majority of the boobies who listened to him, more especially those with no votes.

The election woke up ever-sleepy Dudsworth, provoking it into a mild state of enthusiasm, but it was not until the morning of the polling day that the lion really shook his mane and roared.

Early on that morning Mr. Lawson drove into the town in a carriage and pair, accompanied by his three daughters, radiant with yellow bonnet-strings. The representative of the Great Liberal Party was trotting down High Street very respectably, when in rattled Sir Harry Frankwell, driving four-in-hand, the roof of his drag covered with half a dozen of Gilbert's brother officers, the inside lit up with four of the prettiest faces, arrayed in blue, that ever gazed upon an unenfranchised working man.

Sir Harry's drag, with its living ornaments, had its effect, and the cheers with which it was greeted meant winning, he said.

Mr. Lawson took the applause very composedly,

for he felt sure that if he had rattled in with four, instead of with a pair of horses, that he would been similarly honoured.

Sir Harry believed thoroughly in the force of effect, and he pounded his four bays up and down the streets of Dudsworth for an hour.

At ten o'clock the first return of the poll was announced, and the numbers showed—

Lawson - - - - 71
Frankwell - - - 49

" That looks devilish bad," said Sir Harry ; " first blood for Lawson ;" and off he went with his drag, that being his sole idea of canvassing.

The possibility of being defeated had not once entered his head : the idea of defeat was incompatible with the confidence his natural goodness of spirits inspired. He got a little nervous, however, when the state of the poll, at eleven o'clock, showed—

Lawson - - - 195
Frankwell - - - 106

" By Jove, I must have some champagne."

The fact of the matter was, that the strength of the Liberals not having been tested for so many years, the leading members of their own, and of the Tory party had no very accurate idea what that strength really was now.

Mr. Lawson was the first Dudsworth man who had come forward for years, and he was supported now because he was local as well as Liberal.

He was getting on at this election, if anything, rather better than he had expected, and when the twelve o'clock polling was announced, the three daughters, with the yellow bonnet strings, saw visions of three members of Parliament serenading them under the windows of the contemplated house in Wilton Place.

Sir Harry just returned from a lively drive as the numbers were being put up, and he read—

Lawson - - - 347

Frankwell - - - 203

His exclamation on reading the above would not look pretty in print, so it must be left to the ever-vivid imagination of the intelligent reader.

Sir Harry instantly mounted his drag with the intention of driving back to the castle, and remaining there. Such a proceeding, however, he was told, would be construed into a show of the white feather, and that many of his supporters would, in consequence, not take the trouble to record their votes.

So he rattled through the town again, coming back to his hotel at one o'clock to luncheon.

Until Nellie's elopement Sir Harry had not known the meaning of depression; he could not fancy the opposite feeling to that which he had enjoyed all his life hitherto—hilarity: now, though the election was not lost, he was in a dungeon of despair. He cared nothing about the election now; the sooner Mr. Lawson was returned the better. A week ago there was no place in the world like the House of Commons: now he told one of his pretty blue-bonneted cousins, he would not care if the house were burnt down, and every member singed!

"But, Harry, you've not lost yet."

"My dear Bessie, you are very pretty, and your eyes thrash your blue bonnet strings into fits, but you know nothing about elections. I'm licked, though I don't know why I ought to be. I'm a sinner, of course; you know that well enough,

Bessie, don't you ? but really I don't see the force of being punished so awfully as by being licked on my own property. The one o'clock polling will be out directly ; that will be the crisis."

"Well, let us go and see the crisis."

"No, let the crisis come to us : I'm not going to meet Satan half-way."

The crisis was presently handed to Sir Harry, and he read—

Lawson   -   -   -. 473
Frankwell -   -   -   396

"Tell them they need not keep the poll open any longer, Mr. Gnokes : it's no use, I can't win now. It's deuced shabby of those Dudsworth brutes not to vote for me. Here I've lived amongst them over six hundred years, my grandfather, father, and that sort of people included, and they prefer a man of whose existence they were not aware twenty years ago. Close the poll : I shall shut up and go home."

Of course, no notice was taken of these orders, but not all Bessie's pretty persuasion, not all Gilbert and his military friends could say, not all the entreaties of Mr. Gnokes and the committee could induce Sir Harry to stay any longer in the town.

He went off a few minutes after one, not in the drag, but quietly in a cab. His last orders were, "Tool the drag about, Gil, if you think there's half a chance : I think there's none, but tool it." To this drag Sir Harry had nailed, screwed, and rivetted his faith, feeling convinced that it would be a most effectual canvasser in a good Tory borough ; even it had failed, apparently ; every hope, therefore, was gone, and our excitable friend felt there was nothing left for him but to go home.

"Put your feet in hot water," "Take a glass of iced gruel," "Go and bruise your oats," "Double up your perambulator," with other like pieces of advice, formed the style of consolation Sir Harry got from his immediate friends. But he took no notice of anybody or anything: he lit a cigar, leaned back in the cab, and was quietly driven to the castle.

When he reached home, he went into his own little room, sacred to the paintings of racers, hunters, and cricketing celebrities, together with a sprinkling of theatrical, operatic, and *ballet* grandees; and up and down he walked in a state of most desponding depression.

All seemed to be going wrong.

A few weeks ago he had lost Nellie; now he was losing the election.

Up till the loss of Nellie he had commanded his own world, now he was being knocked about by every world, and most undeservedly.

Ninety-nine men out of a hundred would have stuck to the polling place to the last, and on no account have given up all hopes because they had a minority of seventy-seven at one o'clock. Sir Harry expected to lead from the first; all his life he had expected to lead from the first in pretty well everything, and to a great extent he had so led until he fell in love.

He considered himself the most cruelly treated man alive.

All his pluck and spirits had vanished; he walked up and down his room, feeling nervous and disappointed.

Had this been his first rebuff, he would probably have taken matters differently; now he was sore from the wound Nellie had inflicted; this disappointment opened that great wound, and made the sufferer writhe. Presently he rang the bell.

" Bring me a bottle of champagne, Biggs."

This was one of his infallible remedies, as we are aware ; but he knew that it could only put him straight for a short time ; a smoke, however, might help him on till the return of his brother, cousins, and friends.

No one in the world enjoyed life more than our friend Sir Harry when the world was treating him welf, and no one suffered more when it ill-treated him.

He had told Gilbert in confidence that positively Nellie had given him quite a turn for girls ; and now as he walked up and down his room in wretched loneliness, he felt that he only wanted a comforter—a feminine one preferred—to put him a little straight. His noisy friends were no use to him in such an emergency ; what he wanted was a quiet gentle girl, who would admit that it was a great shame for the Dudsworth folks to vote against him, and comfort him with her sympathy, taking half of his disgust upon her own pretty shoulders.

" Well, if I'm to be badly served in this way another time, I won't go through the agony alone. I'll have a sublime girl with me ; one I can love, one who will be a somebody to cheer a fellow up when this hideous world knocks him down. I'll marry ; it will be an excitement, and one, by Jove, that will last for life ; yes, I'll marry an animate bottle of champagne, one that a fellow can't empty till he's done for himself."

This thought put a little colour into the cheeks of his heart ; and three glasses of the veritable sparkling fluid brushed him up.

It was two o'clock as he tossed off the third glass; and had he been in Dudsworth at that moment, he would have found the state of the poll to be

Lawson, - - - 549
Frankwell, - - 489

Neither Gilbert Frankwell nor any one of the Tory party had despaired of Sir Harry's return. At two o'clock matters were looking up, and Gilbert felt half inclined to take the drag to the castle to cheer the would-be Member. He determined, however, to wait till three o'clock, an hour which all felt would virtually decide the contest.

The anxious time at length arrived, and the numbers stood—

Lawson, - - - 591
Frankwell, - 547

"It's all up," exclaimed Gilbert; an opinion, be it understood, which he formed solely from the above return.

At half-past three, Sir Harry ordered his dog-cart round, determined himself to see the last return at four.

He could not remain longer in the house. He was getting very nervous, and while he dreaded the worst, he longed to know it for certain.

He drove as far as the first large public-house, in one of whose windows he saw a copy of the three o'clock return.

"It's gone agin you, Sir Arry," said an idler standing by; "but there's bin a tidy bit o' bribing goin' on. I myself see'd five ten pun' noats give away the last twenty minutes; for they do say as Mr. Lawson polled his last man at five minutes to three. Jakes o' the Red Lion, however, says as

Mr. Lawson is too far ahead to be beat 'tween this and four."

"I don't care if he has doubled me fifty times over, or if he gives five hundred pounds a vote every twenty minutes. Read me that return in the window."

The man read it, and instantly Sir Harry wheeled round, and drove back to the castle as fast as the animal could take him.

Now was he plunged into a second fit of depression; he had just allowed himself to fancy that there was the possibility of his being four or five ahead at three o'clock, and, lo! he found himself many votes behind. He was quite done for now; he was unquestionably the most ill-used man alive; he would leave Dudsworth to-morrow, shut up the castle, or sell it to a soap-boiler, sugar-baker, to anybody, in fact, rich enough to be nobody!

He sat down in his commodious sofa-chair, threw himself back, and let his miserable thoughts chase themselves hither and thither in his miserable mind.

"It's the only thing to save my life," he exclaimed after awhile; "it's a case of dying or marrying, and, hang it, marrying at the worst of times ought to be better than dying. I'll marry; I'll have a crinoline always by me to do consolation, and pick up the pieces when I'm knocked about like this."

For a quarter of an hour he was in a reverie, his body at Dudsworth, his mind far away. His thoughts tried to wander to Nellie, but he rapidly brought them down upon their haunches, and wheeled them off in an opposite direction.

He was startled into active life by the sound of horses' feet in the park.

Getting up, he saw the drag approaching at ultra four-in-hand speed.

"Confound it, Gil needn't bucket those horses about in that way to tell me I'm thrashed."

His first idea was to go into the hall and brave out the bad news; his second to sit still and not meet the devil half-way.

In a couple of minutes Satan opened the door, and with a very bright happy face said to him, "Harry, permit me to congratulate you."

"Bessie," he said, getting up and taking hold of his cousin's primrose kid hand: "Bessie, if you were a man I would knock you down for chaffing me. My dearly beloved cousin, how you would pity me if you did but know the agony I have endured this day. Toothache is nothing to it, headache a luxury, measles an appetizer. Oh, Bessie, I have been cruelly knocked about, so cruelly that I am in hopes I have been atoning for past somewhat numerous iniquities by suffering in *this* world. I have read, smoked, and imbibed, and I have resolved to take unto myself that most horrible of plagues or most delicious of blessings, a wife. Bessie, you would suit me exactly; but I presume you would not throw over Bob Howard. Let me compliment you by saying that I don't believe you would be a plague; oh no! I don't fancy that for a moment; on the contrary, you would be more or less a blessing, just as temper or fancy might decide; but you would be quite enough of a blessing for me. It would not do to have a wife *too* delightful, you know, or a fellow would be apt to forget his male friends, his dogs, horses, tailor, the Derby, Doncaster, &c. &c.; you would not be too delightful, and therefore would just suit me. And, Bessie——"

H

" Now, I will hear no more rubbish ; read this."
Whereupon Sir Harry tore open an envelope,
and read—

Close of the Poll.
Frankwell   -   -   703
Lawson   -   -   -   641

" Bessie, my prettiest of cousins, you have saved
my life ! Yes, I must have one ; Bob is nowhere
near ;" saying which, Sir Harry in his towering
enthusiasm kissed his preserver, greatly to her
astonishment.

Mr. Lawson had polled his last man a few
minutes after three o'clock, at the moment when
Sir Harry's supporters were coming in with a rush.
Many more blow-hot blow-cold ones could have
been had if they had been wanted, many who held
aloof not wishing to vote either way, as they had a
great personal liking for Mr. Lawson, and did not
wish to vote against him. Had there been any
real doubt as to Sir Harry's chance of success they
would have voted for him to a man.

Sir Harry might have known this, and fifty other
matters connected with the election and its probable
result, had he taken the trouble to ask. But no, he
would take no trouble, he would leave all that
to his agent and committee. Again and again they
had told him that the Tories on the register num-
bered nearly two hundred more than the opposite
side, but that the men required looking up. Sir
Harry, however, had no idea of any but a most
decidedly *otium cum dig.* candidature, and so he contented himself with jerking out a few speeches, with
shutting up an occasional " voice," tooling his drag
about, and feeling over-confident. That was his
nature.

When he found that he did not lead the poll from the first he believed all lost, and nothing that Mr. Gnokes could say was able to change his belief.

A few minutes after his cousin had brought the welcome news, and had been paid in Cupid's coin, Gilbert Frankwell, Lord Huntingsdale, and the other Guardsmen came into the room.

" Ring the bell, Gil."

Gilbert knew well what this command would lead to, so when a footman made his appearance he said, " A glass of water for Sir Harry."

" Take six bottles of champagne into the dining-room, Thomas, three bottles of Bass, and some ice. Bessie, do you know what champagnigaff is ? it's the first tipple going ; one third of Clicquot to two-thirds of Bass, mix and drink.   It seems an insult to cham. to join it with so vulgar a concoction as beer, but the result is simply magnificent.   Now, then, go into the dining-room, my noble friends ; stand not upon the order of your going, but go and be hung to you.   Ha ! ha !   Shakespere.   Now for a toast.   Life and health to Lord Derby : everlasting measles to the Liberals !   By the way, Hunty, if our classical friend Horace had ever read my lord's Homer, I think he would have struck out that line of his, *quandoque bonus dormitat Homerus.*"

" Why ?"

" Why ?   Because I think that *nunquam dormio* is more to our noble friend's taste.   Ha ! ha !   By Jove, I'll say that in the House some night !"

CHAPTER IX.

A SAD NIGHT'S WORK.

MR. AND MRS. ARCHIBALD LORFORD had settled in Scotland; they had taken a small house not far from Stirling, and were now living therein in blissful quiet.

There is no country in the world better adapted to the requirements of English elopers than bonnie Scotland. It is completely in the world, yet a delightful distance from that particular part of the world in which the elopement took place. In Scotland you are nearly sure to be a nice distance from the bride's relatives, about whom you probably care very little, and you feel that you have your wife as completely to yourself as if you had taken her to Iceland, Elba, or Llanfairpwlgwyngwl.

Archibald felt now that he had Nellie entirely to himself, that he had married her and her alone, and that when it was necessary to manifest a little dutifulness to the mother, this might be done through the accommodation offered by the Postmaster-general.

Allansay Lodge was built in one of the loveliest spots that bonnie Scotland can boast, a fact which says a great deal. It was situated about two hundred yards from the high road in little charming grounds of its own, amidst gardens laid out with exquisite taste, and shrubberies the very poetry of shade and seclusion.

It was in all points a fit spot for the enjoyment of such happiness as was bound to spring from the love of our worthy eloping friends.

Who can doubt Nellie's multifarious perfections as a wife?

Who can question Archibald Lorford's goodness and devotedness as a husband?

I very confidently write, no one.

Would that I could pause and dilate upon the happiness of one of the happiest couples this ill-tempered world ever contained, but pause I dare not; dilate I must not. Time presses not, but space.

Two years of happiness that knew no alloy, that bade fair to increase month by month, were passed in this pleasant little home.

A little son made rather a noisy appearance a few months after our friends arrived at Allansay Lodge, and a smart, sturdy, young Life-guardsman he was.

In course of time he was followed by a brother, who perhaps would have been a little mite more acceptable had he been a sister.

There is, however, no centipede, quadruped, biped, or other ped in the world more perverse than the little stranger. When we are dying for a little lady, a little gentleman comes, and when we want a little gentleman, to whom perhaps we hold out the attraction of being an heir, three or four little ladies come one after another with most charming innocence and perversity.

Yet we cannot have too many of them be they what they may, for there never was a large family yet, which, if well brought up, did not turn out well, far better indeed than ten thousand small ones.

There is more happiness, a good many of us

think, in having a quiver half full than entirely full, but who can say when the quiver *is* full? Quivers differ in size. Archibald Lorford thought that with four hundred a year his might be well considered full with three arrows; two, as it happened, filled it.

To add to the general perversity of his nature, the little stranger sometimes fixes upon very bad weather for his nativity, and this was the case with the second Master Lorford. He was born on a stormy, tempestuous night in January, and Archibald had cause to be greatly alarmed on his mother's account. The awful storm terrified her and made her feverish, and as the new comer was not expected just at present, poor Nellie was without the medical aid of that eminent man, Mr. Carruthers.

Archibald sat by her side for two hours, unable to make up his mind to go, and yet knowing that either he or some messenger ought to be on his way to Stirling for medical assistance.

About one o'clock in the morning he determined to leave Nellie under the care of Mrs. Weedow, a valuable, trustworthy old servant, and drive off at once to the town.

He went into the stable yard, put the pony, which was unluckily too small to ride, into Nellie's little carriage, and started off.

He could not resist the temptation of taking one more look at the patient sufferer before finally quitting the house. When he entered the room he found her really asleep, but as he thought insensible, and when he closed the door and hurried off to the pony carriage, he believed that he would never see her again alive.

He felt sure that Nellie was dying, and all perhaps for the want of medical care.

Never did man drive on with such desperation as did Archibald Lorford now.

It was a case of life and death, and he believed that the scales were turning in favour of the latter.

Added to the stormy raging of wind and rain was the maddening hindrance of the almost impenetrable darkness.

In blind desperation, Archibald drove on, every now and then within an ace of upsetting the little carriage by his inability to keep the centre of the road.

Had there been any man, horse, or vehicle coming in an opposite direction, there must inevitably have been a collision.

Archibald really could not see a yard before him.

In his hurry he had come away without lamps, and indeed had he had time to think of them, he would have been unable to find them, as the old man who attended to the pony had locked them up, and gone to his home, a mile or two off, hours ago.

Seven long miles had Archibald Lorford to drive ere he could reach the house of the nearest doctor. His pony, a most willing one, went well; but it did not stand over thirteen hands, and knowing the necessity for the highest possible rate of speed, Archibald's agony was increased as he felt that but for the comparative slowness of the animal, he might now have been so much, and so much farther on his way. This thought worried him every yard of these seven weary miles, and more than once he half determined to pull up and run on foot by a slightly nearer way across some fields.

He had gone four miles when the pony suddenly stopped, and despite much lashing and coaxing refused to move an inch. Archibald got out and found that the little burn between Allansay and Stirling had, by reason of the recent rains, over-flowed its banks, and was now on a level with the rustic wooden bridge that here crossed it.

He had nothing to do but to leave the pony and carriage on one side of the road, and make the best of his way ahead through the stream.

It was now rushing with impetuous force. Every moment seemed to swell it; the rush of its torrent was terrific, for it seemed at least six times its usual width and depth, and thrice Archibald was carried off his legs ere he gained the road on the opposite side.

Three more miles had he to go yet; he ran, walked, ran, walked as fast as he could lay foot to ground, seriously impeded by his dripping clothes, and every now and then obliged to stop and listen when he fancied he heard sounds of some person or animal approaching.

And listening was no easy matter.

The beating of the heavy rain upon the ground, and the way in which it was lashed by the vehemence of the wind through the trees, made an in-cessant tumultuous roar, leaving him to fancy that he was rushing through some wild deserted country, wherefrom the violence of the elements had driven all but himself.

Not a creature did he meet in his long and weary journey; scarce a sound did he hear but that mono-tonous roar which the storminess of the night pro-duced.

On, on till fresh impediment stayed him.

At the end of his first mile after crossing the burn, he found that nearly the whole distance must be re-traversed; he had struck out of the high road and gone down a little lane, whose ending was a farmhouse now unoccupied.

Back again all that weary way; the thought that Nellie might even now be dead, or that medical help at this very moment could alone save her, maddening him so as rather to lessen than increase his speed.

Nellie was sensible now, she was better; yet the woman who watched by her side hesitated to tell her young mistress that Archibald was out in the midst of this fearful storm, the violence of which sounded only too plainly in Nellie's room.

Her new little boy was making a horrible noise, which even his good mother was too ill to enjoy.

Again did Archibald Lorford find himself by the swollen stream, and again did he start from it, and this time in the right road for Stirling. So utterly wearied was he that he all but despaired of ever getting over the three miles that lay between him and the surgeon.

Not one atom did the storm abate that fearful night, and when it was about at its height Archibald set foot upon the paved streets of Stirling. At length he reached the house of Mr. Carruthers, and after knocking and ringing for five minutes, burst the door open with a vigorous kick, and rushed upstairs.

In making for the doctor, Archibald Lorford had to make for his beard, for in no other way could he distinguish him in the darkness.

As ill luck ruled, the first room he entered was that occupied by the doctor's grandmother, a very old lady, and it is no figure of speech to say that he nearly frightened her to death, when he laid his hand upon her face, to ascertain if the object of his search, the beard, were there. She shrieked and screamed as no *man* could have, and Archibald hurried away after a very incomplete facial investigation.

Happily, the next face upon which he laid his hand possessed a beard, and there could be no doubt, therefore, that it was the doctor's. The worthy Scotchman was very easily awoke, and took but little time to make out the object of this unexpected visit.

" I would not turn a dog out in a night like this, I confess, Mr. Carruthers ; but my wife—my wife, she is dy——she is——"

"Ye need mak' no apology to a king, Mr. Lorford, for turning him oot if he were a medical man. I'll be up in a second. Will ye have the goodness to give that bell three shairp pulls ? I thank ye ; and will ye noo go down stairs and tell my man, when he comes, to put Wallace in the gig ?"

And the doctor got up, hurriedly dressed himself, spent a few minutes in his surgery, and then started off with Archibald in the gig, which had been brought round with astonishing rapidity.

The doctor and his man were used to being called up in the night, and custom had sharpened the natural quickness of their movements.

Rightly to judge of this fearful night, it was necessary to go into the open air. Mr. Carruthers had looked out of his window, and hoped that Archibald had rather exaggerated the state of affairs. Far from it.

Not only would you not wish to turn a dog out, but if, contrary to your wish, you did turn one out, most assuredly you would not expect ever to see his faithful tail wag again.

Mr. Carruthers had not gone a quarter of a mile before both lamp candles were blown out, and not a hundred yards farther before the lamps themselves were shaken by successive violent gusts of wind, and eventually thrown into the road, and smashed to pieces.

Neither the doctor nor Archibald Lorford spoke a word, and had either attempted, the voice would have been inaudible ; but neither had the inclination to talk.

The doctor was well accustomed to night-work, and knew every inch of the road he was going ; but it was all he could do to make out his way and keep the horse straight.

Archibald Lorford was all thought one moment, all fear the next, and all hope the next; at least he tried very hard to be all hope.

He fancied that two years ago he had known pretty well the agony of mind which is inevitable when love matters go wrong, and he had come to the conclusion that no mental pain is as acute as that which arises from love's disappointments.

A refusal begets torture of mind indescribable, and, as the rejected one thinks, is not to be exceeded.

This Archibald had not tasted ; but, at a time when he was desperately in love, he had lost sight of Nellie for months, and when next he heard of her, it was as the bride-elect of Sir Harry Frankwell. There was plenty of torture in this, and, at the time, he thought nothing could beat it.

He was beginning to think differently at this moment.

It is a bald idea of love that men have before marriage. They fancy themselves on fire, they believe that passionate adoration in its intensity can no further go, but in reality the fevered combination of sensations, which glowing affection, restlessness, nervousness and anxious longing produce, are but the sherry and bitters, or oysters to whet the appetite for that feast of mind and soul which exists for years after the celebration of a happy marriage.

" Love comes after marriage," is one of the tritest of phrases, but one more heavily weighted with solid, incontrovertible truth was never uttered.

The love we feel during courtship is, at best, but the shadow cast before by the coming events of a happy union : or else it is an insignificant light of itself, which may go out with the end of the court·ship.

There may be few bachelors, perhaps, who believe this, for do not numbers think that the ante-matrimonial love to which their friends on all sides fall victims, is love of a very high order, and not in fact to be exceeded ?

Not one married man on earth, happily mated, is there, who would not willingly grow hoarse in his endeavour to testify to the truth of the trite, old phrase quoted above.

L'amitié est l'amour sans ailes, so ante-matrimonial love is but an exaggerated form of close friendship, love without wings.

To this universal doctrine amongst married men Archibald Lorford had most heartily subscribed. The love he felt for Nellie whilst quietly wooing her, seemed as nothing beside what lay within his very soul these two years of married life

Wooers who stick up for short, sharp, and decisive courtships are wont to say, " Bless you, my dear fellow, I shall know as much about Jessie in six weeks as I should if I had made love to her for six years." And he who so says is pretty nearly right, for he will know next to nothing at all about Jessie if he woo her most persistently for the whole of the six years. Love *making* cannot possibly enable him to see more than the mere outline of Jessie's character: he cannot take in her real character, and see it in all its glory, until he and she have put their wings on. Nevertheless, his aggravated form of intense friendship is quite sufficiently strong to lead him to be pretty sure that when he knows Jessie's character after matrimony, he will have the felicity of losing himself in positive adoration, in wing'd love.

Long courtships and engagements are futile torture in many instances, especially if one of their objects be to try and find out the beauties, devotedness, and myriad jewels of disposition and nature before marriage.

Only let the wings be fastened on by that all-holding little golden ring, and after it has been worn but a very few months, then will come out, in all its wondrous light, that post-matrimonial insight into character, that reciprocity of limitless confidence which wedded folks know to be the leavening ingredient in the marvellous composition of love!

How much of this composition do we really see in courtship? A particle perhaps, beside which, a grain of white sand might hold up its head.

A hundred times had Archibald Lorford fancied when, years ago, he was making quiet love to little Nellie Branston, that he was getting glimpses of the beauty of her character, and that when she opened her heart to him, he was enjoying a bite of the golden grape of confidence which forms the wine of the tipsy-cake of matrimony.

By placing confidence in a man, a girl, as all the world knows, binds the lord of creation to her, and pays him a compliment, which, taken as a compliment only, is superior to the honour she does him in accepting his hand, heart, pin-money, town and country house, barouche, brougham, drag, chestnut hunter, &c., &c. !

But how can this confidence be given to any great extent when he and she are *sans ailes ?*

These were thoughts that rattled through Archibald Lorford's troubled mind as he was driven hurriedly along, and these and those that followed drove him all but into a frenzy.

He had been prostrated with what he thought overwhelming grief when, two years ago, he believed he had lost Nellie, and then he only saw and knew her by the insignificant light of ante-matrimonial love.

Now he was finding the very suspicion of losing her, for he could not believe that he had actually lost her, all but unbearable.

He had enjoyed her confidence, he had noted the countless charms of her character these two years, and now therefore he had some idea of the loss that might possibly fall upon him.

All the adorableness of her character he had, of course, failed to discover before marriage, well as he thought he knew her, and so, had he lost her two years ago, he would not have had then one hundredth part of the agony and pain that would fall upon him now.

He was almost insensible with the raging storm of prospective grief that was now going on within him. He knew that he was moving along, and pretty rapidly too, but he took no heed of roar of wind and splash of rain.

He was too much absorbed in agonising thought to be able to warn his companion of the danger that was inevitable if they got into the torrent-sweep of the swollen stream, its banks now overflowed beyond doubt to a far greater extent than they were two hours ago.

Barely distinguishable was its impetuous, whirling rush, amidst the beating of the rain and the howling of the wind. The burn was running at fearful pace, volumes of water hurled along at almost the speed of a cataract.

And Archibald Lorford and the doctor were now within thirty yards of its edge, hurrying on with the utmost rapidity.

CHAPTER X.

LIFE OR DEATH?

NELLIE was infinitely better; she was showing un-
mistakable signs of coming round, and within the
last half hour Mrs. Weedow had ventured to tell her
the cause of Mr. Lorford's absence on this awful
night. She had not said how long he had been
away, and Nellie, happily, did not inquire. To
conceal from her the fearfulness of the storm was
impossible, for, as I have before said, the noise of
its roar and tumult sounded too plainly in Nellie's
own room. Her own danger she very soon forgot,
but her anxiety on her husband's behalf rapidly
increased to an extent which alarmed her nurse.

Nellie was too weak to speak much, but a few
words every now and then escaped her, her face
showing the intensity of her anxiety on Archibald's
account, an anxiety she expressed whenever she
felt strong enough to ask her nurse of the night.

The tears began to flow as time wore on and no
tidings of Archibald came. To see him now would
be the surest means of hastening her recovery, and
his absence, she felt, was keeping her back.

At first she had not thought of him being in
danger, but gradually this idea had stolen in upon
her mind, and she became restless, nervous, and
painfully anxious.

She listened with strained attention for the
sound of his footsteps upon the stairs, and through
more than an hour she listened in vain.

She fondled and handled her little son with that infinite, marvellous, and skilful gentleness which seems to forsake no mother, let her condition be what it may ; but even he, great though he was in his preciousness, could not divert her thoughts for two minutes together.

Sleep was a merciful relief.

Hitherto, since marriage, Archibald and Nellie Lorford had sailed life s ocean in a calm.

This was the first storm that had burst over Allansay Lodge, the first occasion on which all had not gone smoothly for our now weather-beaten friends.

Not even a poet's fancy could picture purer peacefulness and quietude of life than had been enjoyed by Archibald and Nellie up to this day of storms within and without; the fancy of no poet could rightly tell the wondrous greatness of the change this unhappy illness within and awful wrath of nature without had brought about.

Husband and wife separated, and each in imminent danger; two separated who had hitherto been virtually one, who dreamt not of danger in the security and providence that seemed everywhere to surround them.

They were neither fore-armed nor fore-warned; their first danger and trouble came upon them with a crash.

And so would the chief of troubles fall upon the whole world were sudden death the rule instead of the great exception.

Sickness, oft or but once repeated, graduates the grief of sufferer, sympathiser, and mourner; it ever beckons to fortitude and resignation, forewarning them that the end may be such as shall require the highest exercise of all their powers.

But Archibald and Nellie had had no sickness, so to say; there had been nothing to beckon to their powers of endurance during these two happy years.

For three hours Nellie's eyes were closed. It was now the nurse's turn to be anxious, inasmuch as she feared that much sleep might be a bad rather than a good sign. But such was not the case; Nellie was sleeping soundly, and though she awoke with a sudden start, she awoke refreshed and invigorated.

She started, for she heard the sound of footsteps on the stairs.

Her pale face brightened; she drew her little one more closely to her, and awaited with feelings of joyful hope the opening of the door.

She waited but half a minute; the door was opened, but he who entered the room was not Archibald Lorford.

It seemed strange that Mr. Carruthers should not see the imminence of the danger as he approached the rushing torrent; strange, because his eyes had become somewhat accustomed to the darkness of the night.

As I have before said, he was well used to night work; he had driven many miles by night, but never through such darkness as this, and he had not once met with accident of any description.

To-night he had miscalculated the distance he had gone; he believed himself at least a quarter of a mile from the wooden bridge over the burn. As for Archibald Lorford, he was insensible to everything but his anxiety for, and fear about, Nellie.

The roar of the rushing waters would have sounded thunder-like had it not been for the vio-

lent raging of wind and rain ; as it was, it seemed
but to swell the tumult that had accompanied the
two from Stirling, and did not therefore attract
the doctor's special attention. The additional roar
he necessarily observed, but believing himself some
way yet from the bridge, he did not for a moment
attribute it to the overflow and sweep of the stream.

The danger was at hand ; the doctor saw it, but
not until it was too late.

As his eye caught sight of the sweeping waters,
his horse was swung off his legs, and in another
second the gig was hurled down the stream.

In another moment, the gig being overturned,
the doctor and Archibald Lorford were struggling
in the heart of the current.

The doctor was as strong and powerful a man as
Archibald, and, what stood him in good stead now,
he was an excellent swimmer. Yards from him on
the right, he could hear a voice faintly exclaim,
" Go on, doctor, go on, for mercy's sake ; don't
wait for anything if you can cross. I am all right ;
can you cross ? are you over ? Go on, doctor, go
on ; you'll be saved, you'll be saved ; don't think
of any one but yourself ; don't wait for me ; leave
me alone, I'm all right. Oh, my wife ! my wife !
Have you crossed ? Oh, my wife ! my wife ! Are
you over ? are you   "

It was a hard battle the doctor fought with the
fearful torrent into which he had been plunged.
Strength and desperation fought for him ; the natural struggle for life gave him giant power ; irre-
sistible determination nerved him, and the manli-
ness that defies fear urged him stoutly on.

He had crossed.

He knew not whether, as he landed safely, to go
to the assistance of Archibald, who, for all he knew,

might be in the greatest danger, or whether to make at once for Allansay.

He called out at the top of his voice to his companion.

Archibald, apparently but a few yards from him, answered, " Go on, doctor, go on, I pray you ; I shall be over in two minutes."

The doctor hesitated to go and leave Archibald struggling in the stream.

" Are you there, doctor ? "

" Yes."

" Oh ! go ; I pray you go ; I am over ; I am on the bank."

And the doctor hurried rapidly away.

He followed the stream as well as he was able, and presently reached the road.

He had just started to run when he almost stumbled over what proved to be Nellie's pony carriage.

It was empty, he saw. He called aloud three or four times to arouse any one that might own it, for he was not aware to whom it belonged, and receiving no answer, got into it, took the reins in hand, and set off the pony, cold and wet though the poor animal was, at a smart gallop.

His own gig and horse were not carried far before they got on to a high bank in a field ; up this the animal struggled and so saved himself and his master's property.

Archibald Lorford was not so fortunate ; for a second after the doctor left him, the strength of the current carried him down fully a hundred yards, and he had no power to make a single stroke towards either bank.

He had told the doctor he was over, but merely that he might hasten him away ; at the moment of saying so he was in mid-stream, struggling violently, and it was only by an effort, of which he scarcely believed himself capable, that he could muster strength sufficient to cry out that he was on the bank. If ever a lie were justifiable, surely this one was.

His violent struggles continued, but in a while he was driven with tremendous force against a tree which had fallen half way across the stream. He clung to it with all the strength left in him, the water sweeping by with terrific force, each rush loosening the little hold he had obtained.

The torrent would not allow him to creep on to the tree or he might have worked his way up it on to the bank; in a short while it swept him off and bore him away at fewest another hundred yards.

Here he was stopped by some stout wooden railings which ran across the burn, and by the exercise of all his remaining strength, and oh! how little that was, he managed to get hold of the top rail, and eventually to raise himself on to it.

Here he felt comparatively safe, and now that he had saved himself his thoughts flew homewards.

How was Nellie! would he see her again alive? Would the doctor be in time to save her? And then, as he asked those questions, came that fearful exertion of the memory by which it reviews for us in a minute the happiness and troubles of a life-time.

His first meeting with Nellie rose like a picture before him. How well he remembered her as a little girl! how well he remembered the first day he saw her after his first parting; how well the time when his heart told him he was beginning to love this little fascinating beauty. All her childish speeches came into his mind; his leave-taking when he was about to start on diplomatic service abroad; his return; his intense admiration of the fine, comely, well-grown girl he now met at the rectory; the quiet walks and conversations together, and the temporary separation on the rector's death; the meeting many months afterwards, and each and every event that happened to them both since the opening chapter of this history; all these memories passed as it were in pictures before him, and a hundred other recollections of a not uneventful life. And memory did its worst in flashing as lightning before him errors and frailties which are, as we hope, however great, well within the limits of a pardon that man's judgment dictates not.

He was startled from his reverie; his safety was but fancied.

The railing whereon he had sat, to which rather he had clung, suddenly shook beneath him; the waters roared along as it seemed with increasing force, and swept him backwards into their fearful torrent.

Backwards he was hurled with terrific violence, his head dashed against the huge stones that lay beneath him.

He was stunned; his strong limbs were powerless; he sank to the bottom of the stream; he rose but for a moment, and then his lifeless body was borne rapidly away!

*   *   *   *   *

*   *   *   *

CHAPTER XI.

THE PRETTY WIDOW.

FOUR times in the four succeeding weeks had Mr. Carruthers despaired of Nellie Lorford's life, and twice had he summoned Sir George Betleigh, M.D., from Edinburgh, to aid him with his counsel.

To describe Nellie's state of mind during that time, and indeed for months afterwards, were an absolute impossibility, and I will therefore make no attempt.

After a long, tedious, and dangerous illness her bodily health was restored, and about four months after her husband's death, she set out for the south of England, accompanied by her mother and the two boys.

Fill up for yourself, my reader, if you will, the awful sadness of those times which commenced when, after waiting hours and hours for Archibald's return, Nellie overheard a man telling the doctor that Mr. Lorford's *body* had been discovered a mile and a half down the stream. Picture to yourself Nellie's delirium, if you can, that wreck of mental composure which made illness doubly wasting; that unutterable torture of seeing constantly, in fancy, the adored face and form of him who was gone.

To the world she was a widow the instant that lifeless body was hurried down the stream, but it was eighteen long weary months ere her whole nature could acknowledge itself hopelessly widowed, ere her mind could really admit that one to whom she had been so surely wedded was—gone !·

Hastings was the first place to which Nellie was removed on being able to leave Allansay, the paradise of but two years, and four months after she took a little cottage in the neighbourhood of Leeds, where she lived in perfect seclusion.

Now, just twenty months after Archibald's death, we find her with her two boys at Rhyl, North Wales.

I venture to say that nine-tenths of those who have lately made Nellie's acquaintance are right well acquainted with what is fast becoming Manchester *super mare.*

Nellie could not bear a quiet place; she was miserable night and day in her Yorkshire abode, and bathing being necessary for her elder boy, Douglas, she determined to go where she could get life as well as salt-water, and so she fixed upon Rhyl.

She took a little house in Church Street, and prepared herself for a comfortable marine summer.

Four hundred a year was ample for her small establishment, and it enabled her to keep her pony carriage, which she brought with her to Rhyl. In it she drove daily with her two handsome boys, and men, who will be men, called her the "pretty widow." Her mother was not with her. To say truth she was not quite so fond of her as she would like to have been. The widow *mère* was a very heavy companion, intellectually dense, as we know, and amazingly troublesome and fidgetty about the boys of the widow *fille.*

Nellie loved her mother; all Nellies love their mothers, but our Nellie recollected what she looked upon as very great unkindness in days gone by to one who was no more, and whilst she wished to forgive, she knew that to forget was impossible.

Mrs. Branston, moreover, was wanted in London, to provide a home for her son in Messrs. Tutt and

Dangett's bank. The other two were seldom at home, one being at Sandhurst, the other a midshipman, somewhere on the Australian station.

The latter got to Australia, you see, after all, and as he did not go with the idea that he was likely to make money, he formed rather a good opinion of the colonies.

Rhyl is a vastly different place now to what it was not very many years ago. Then it was chiefly frequented by above-stairs society, by county families, by university company, by good parsons with their amiable wives and inevitably large families.

Now, half-way-up-the-stairs society stocks it; Manchester and Liverpool, office and counting-house company, second floor families and the like, with a very sparse sprinkling of the above-stairs persuasion.

Men who are in office at ten o'clock in the morning are on the parade at six P.M. listening to a wheezy band, or mutilating shrimps indoors; and on Sundays and Mondays Birmingham is shovelled wholesalely into the place.

The immortal Jenkins never comes nowadays; he could not breathe the un-Belgravian atmosphere; but Mr. and Mrs. Caudle, Mr. and Mrs. Naggleton and family, Mrs. Brown and the rich relations of policeman X, annually take apartments on East or West Parade!

Fine is the sea, fine are the sands, good the air, free the space; so Rhyl is sure to be patronised, and Nellie was well content to give it her patronage and take from it all she could in the way of health and strength. Nellie enjoyed it, and she bathed her elder boy, and he did not enjoy it probably.

Now men, who will be men, had wondered much

who the pretty widow could be. Fast and loose men were the chief wonderers, and amongst them stood out somewhat prominently a well-off London solicitor.

He thought it quite the right thing to turn up unexpectedly a dozen times a day under the pretty widow's nose, and to pat the bathing boy occasionally on the head as he passed.

Nellie began to hate the sight of him.

"If you ever see that gentle—— that man coming, Mary," she said to the Masters Lorford's nurse, "tell me; I do not wish to meet him; he is an exceedingly rude and forward person."

Duly warned, Nellie often escaped the solicitor after the issuing of the above order.

Not so the nurse. She thought the solicitor a nice gentleman, and had quite enough impudence to return one of his studied smiles.

"My word, that's a fine little fellow you are carrying, nurse; whose property is he, eh?"

Of this observation Mary took no notice, and she passed by him somewhat quickly, not even turning round to look at him.

He was far too nice, however, in her eyes, to be thus treated a second time.

A day or two after, when they met again, the lawyer addressed himself directly to Mary, making no allusion to the boy in her arms; and there being no one within a hundred yards or so, he sat by her side on a bench, and won her heart with a few of his Londonisms.

He knew how to talk to his audience, and his audience very soon gave him the name of the pretty widow.

"Any relation to Lawford, the wholesale stationer in Cannon Street?"

Now Mary's dignity was offended.

"Master was a gentleman," she replied.

"Oh! yes, yes, of course; and, by the way, Sarah—I am sure your name is Sarah. No? Well, I am astonished—is she pretty well off?"

Mary thought she was very well off.

"And tell me, pretty Susan—not Susan? Dear me, what a muff I am to-day; tell me, has she any gentlemen visitors here?"

Not *as* Mary was aware of.

"Oh! but you must know, Mary. Ah! I am right, it is Mary, ha! ha! ha! Yes, I say you must know, Mary; come, tell me."

A half-crown told him.

"She does not know a creecher in the place, and mopes dreadful when she is alone of an evening."

"Ah! yes, no doubt; laments the dear departed; of course, very natural, very respectable. Any lodgings in your house to let?"

"I've nothing to do with the letting of the lodgings."

"Of course not, of course not; dear me, how you do drop upon me, Mary; you must have been born with a mustard-spoon in your mouth! Come, are there any lodgings to let?"

This was asking too much, and Mary plumply said there were none.

"No? but of course I can see for myself, as I know the house you go into."

This made Mary hot, for she knew that if the lawyer looked up at one of the bow-windows he would see a card therein with "Apartments" thereon.

"There are lodgings, but only for one lady," with which answer Mary cooled herself and her conscience.

In a while the talkers separated, the solicitor saying, half aloud, half to himself, "I should not at all object to supply the place of the dear departed—demme!"

The next day he met Mary and pursued his inquiries, but with little success, for it was little she could tell him. He had bought a ball for Douglas, which Mary would on no account, however, allow him to present; were he to do as he wished, he would set the child a-talking, and the talk would probably not end where it began, but be renewed in the house, and then mischief would follow.

The solicitor, who now fancied himself positively in love, hovered daily about the pretty widow for a week, managing to meet her constantly, but not as yet finding an opportunity of speaking.

Now there was another persistent, and yet not demonstratively persistent, admirer of sweet Nellie in Rhyl at this time. His tactics were the very opposite to those of the Londoner, for though he closely watched fair Nellie, he took care never to be seen himself.

His lodgings were on the East Parade on the ground floor, and the window he usually sat at looked to the front.

This window Nellie passed constantly, and from behind one of the curtains her quiet undemonstrative admirer lovingly watched her.

As she walked along the Parade, it often happened that this admirer was pacing the enclosure, a large space of rough ground lying between the road and the wall which marks the region of sand and beach, and on such occasions the admirer would vault the wall, and, unseen, attentively watch the pretty mourner.

Nellie never saw him, but Mary had noticed the

direction of his eyes on two occasions, for twice she happened to be sitting on the sand near him. Though she certainly considered the solicitor to be a gentleman, she was of opinion that this quiet admirer out-gentlemanised him; and she knew very well that he would put no questions to her of an inquisitive order.

Should he speak to her, she felt that she would necessarily answer him respectfully—not with that familiarity which had come quite naturally to her in replying to the other admirer. But she only thought there was a possibility of him speaking to her, because he had two or three times looked some-what hard at her, or rather at the little boys with her.

He did speak to her, and on this wise. One afternoon, when the tide was out, he was walking quietly along in front of the bathing machines, evidently absorbed in thought. Presently he was slightly startled by hearing the sounds of a little child crying, and looking round he saw Douglas Lorford, with a very woful face, and unmistakable signs of weeping about his large brown eyes.

He at once guessed that the little fellow had lost his nurse, for she was nowhere to be seen, and taking hold of his fat hand, he spoke to and quieted him.

Mary, he could see, was deeply engaged in con-versation with two young men, who to all appear-ance were medical students, or fast clerks of some sort, and apparently they were extracting immense fun out of the baby, whilst they administered ad-miring chaff to the pretty nurse in charge of him.

The quiet admirer seated himself on the steps of a bathing-machine, and put little Douglas upon his knee. His first idea was to take him back at once to his nurse, but on second thoughts he determined to have a brief conversation with the little fellow.

He soon got into conversation with him, and asked him, amongst other things, if mamma sang to him very prettily at night.

" Yes."

" And does she ever sing in an evening for herself, or only for you ?"

"; Only to me and baby."

" And does she ever talk to you about poor papa ?"

" No : I don't 'member poor p'pa."

" Has mamma been very poorly indeed ? "

The little fellow only looked at the quiet admirer, unable apparently to answer the last question. Presently he asked if he might look at the admirer's watch, and permission being readily granted, he took it into his little sandy hands.

Little sandy hands are perhaps ill-suited to the delicate nature of a gold watch, but I feel sure that, to gratify the child, the quiet admirer would have allowed him to bathe the watch in the sea.

" I like 'ou very much, and should like to take our watch home to p'ay with."

" My boy, you should have fifty to play with if I were only able to give them to you : this one, you see, I want to tell me when I ought to go to bed, and when I ought to jump out again."

" Do you jump out of bed ? nurse won't let me."

" Quite right, quite right, it would not do for you to jump out until you are as big as I am. And now, I think, my little fellow, I must take you back to nurse."

" No, no, no, I stop with 'ou."

" I wish you might, my boy. Well, tell me, if I

let you stay with me a bit longer, tell me, does mamma seem very unhappy?"

"No."

"But does she ever laugh and —"

He stopped short, perceiving that the little sandy hands had wrenched open the case of the watch, and that the youngster was far too much engrossed to be able to think about answering questions.

After suggesting that the case had better be closed, as the poor watch might catch cold if it were left open, the quiet admirer took the little fellow back to Mary, not however till he had kissed him a dozen times.

"It would be better," he said, addressing Mary, "if you paid more attention to the children under your care, and listened less to the nonsense of these young men."

These young men looked up at the quiet admirer, and doubtless longed to operate upon his head. The head, however, was a good height from the ground, and appeared to rest upon a pair of shoulders which would hardly look foolish beside a Lord Warden target.

One of them could not help observing, *sotto voce*, as he turned to walk away, "Got an eye on the widow, no doubt," a remark which the quiet admirer unluckily heard—unluckily, for he forthwith administered a terrific box on the right ear, which must have shaken the brains in their pan!

Without saying or doing more, the quiet admirer walked away, and it was several days before Mary saw him again.

A fortnight longer Nellie remained in Rhyl unmolested, enjoying walks and drives, and bathing her boys.

She bathed herself too, and the old dipperess

said she never saw such a young lady for the water, let alone so bonnie a one. Nellie was a perfect Nereid, and though Rhyl has bathed many a mile of long back hair, it never had such a crop of glorious silken streamers in pickle as hers. She looked well in her matronliness, for she was a sturdy, well-made, fresh-looking young widow, and her boys were herself in miniature.

It was impossible not to notice her, as in the bright bloom of health and strength she walked by the sea, or up the little streets of Rhyl. Epithets by the dozen, which find no place in the dictionary of one Johnson, were lavished upon her: epithets which testified to the intensity of masculine admiration, to the slavery of eye-service which beauty entails.

All unconscious of this general admiration, Nellie Lorford enjoyed her marine visit, hating only the solicitor for his conspicuous eye-service.

Her boys were all in all to her; she had few thoughts beyond them.

Her life now was one of infinite quiet, and it seemed unlikely to be ruffled by the least change or excitement. Nellie was too quiet: she was drifting into an unhealthy monotony of life, which threatened to grow oppressive, if not unbearable, as time wore on.

Yet change and excitement would have upset her—so, however, she fancied: but there were times when she felt her sorrow lie very heavily upon her, as there were times when it was as food to her, and even very comfort and consolation.

Let first sorrow be what it may, and no widow in this world felt the fearful laceration of the heart's affections more acutely than Nellie, it cannot last long in its all but insupportable intensity. Time may not cool affection, but it lets in the rays of other warmth which soften the hard front of sorrow, and, as it were, fill up the void by drawing the sides of the open wound together.

It shows no instability of affection and no memory-coolness, when the heart's wounds begin to feel less and less painful: it is purely natural to use all means to effect a cure, when, in the case of mind and heart, sorrow has spent its first force. Resignation grows out of a settling down into the persuasion that as there has been pain, so there must be sorrow, and then from resignation springs up what is not memory-coolness and indifference, but rather the just reward of the good quality of resignation, which is ease and comfort, and that exquisite composure which follows alleviated pain.

Nellie had no one to talk to her, no one who could strive to heal her sorrows, no one who could tell her that she ought to seek out her own comfort and happiness, and not brood over trouble because she would not have her memory behave indifferently to one whom she had loved so well.

Nellie little expected to find new life in Rhyl, but she did find it, and the quietly exciting events of next chapter will show how.

Gentlemen were the last things, or animals rather, that Nellie ever thought of. She was by no means an orthodox young widow, for she hugged her widowhood closely, and almost shuddered at the idea of having it disturbed by masculine attentions. She did not look upon men with the eyes of an old maid: no, her views were far more liberal and enlightened than those held by the orthodox Minerva. She cared nothing about men in fact: she would not climb up a tree to get out of the way of one, as would an old maid proper.

K

Minerva, in a thousand cases, can find no fault with Mr. O'Green, Mr. de Brown, Captain O'Mulligatawnigan, &c., and if you asked her why she disliked so and so, she could only say, " Well, he's a man, you know, which is quite enough for me; he's a man," and so she avoids male company, and builds for herself a Gibraltar of inconnubiality.

Nellie Lorford was no Minerva; it was impossible that she could be one, but nevertheless she hugged her widowhood closely, and avoided gentlemen.

She was not afraid of the stern sex : she would not faint if one invaded the solitude of her railway carriage ; she did not look upon man as a fit object for detention in the Zoos : simply, she did not care sixpence about the sons of Eve. Far be it from me to say that she was a confirmed widow : were I to say that, I should at once announce that she was about to be married. A 'confirmed old maid' is an amiable, estimable lady of sober age, and rickety theological views, who is waiting for an offer : analogically, therefore, we may easily translate the expression, a confirmed widow.

Ladies who say that they are "passionately fond" of music, almost invariably sing *Kafoozalum, Over the Sea, River, river,* and songs of that calibre, and their passionate fondness is merely a drawing-room phrase, which means anything.

With many grains of salt therefore we must believe Miss Goggheogheogan, when she says that she " hates " men, and when her sister declares that Barbara will never marry. It so often happens that the right man is a long time in turning up, and maidens therefore who get the credit for Gibraltarian inconnubiality are cruelly wronged, inasmuch as, poor things, they are only waiting for the waggon : they are pretty sailors whistling for the breeze, and if half a gale of wind comes, of course they don't get what they want, and so they still whistle. But they are not confirmed whistlers : they don't mean to eject shrill sounds of invitation all their lives : half a gale of wind is no more a breeze than that long Mr. Tate is, that short Mr. Bate, who, as it happens, is the right man who *won't* come forward : they only whistle till Mr. Bate turns up.

Do not therefore, my reader, misjudge Nellie Lorford. I simply say that she does not care sixpence about gentlemen ; she prefers widowhood at the present time to conjugal felicity : she is not a 'confirmed widow,' because she has no thought whatever of marrying again. At the same time, as she is a member of that sex of which we never fail to be reminded when we gaze at the summit of a church spire, we must not yet pretend to guess what will be her line of conduct.

> What a strange thing is man ! and what a stranger
> Is woman ! What a whirlwind is her head,
> And what a whirlpool ! .   .
>   Whether wed,
> .   .   Or widow, maid, or mother, she can change her
> Mind like the wind ; whatever she has said
> Or done, is light to what she'll say or do ;—
> The oldest thing on record, and yet new !

CHAPTER XII.

NELLIE'S QUIET ADMIRER.

ONE afternoon, the London solicitor came to the conclusion that his admiration of Nellie had dragged its slow length along, quite long enough, and that he really must speak to her. He would address her quietly and neatly, and he would adopt a little *ruse*.

It was very seldom that Nellie did not make her appearance upon the Parade in a morning about eleven o'clock. She used to set out then after having bathed her boy, if tide had allowed, and administered the mid-day refreshment to himself and his brother.

Usually this refreshment consisted of biscuits, or bread and butter, but on juvenile Saints' days, so to say, it rose to the altitude of cake.

One Monday morning, the solicitor noticed the pretty widow turn out of Church Street along the East Parade, and he noticed, too, that his idol was nearly the only person about.

He overtook her with slightly beating heart, and accidentally, by which I mean intentionally, dropped a glove in front of her. Of course, he had to turn round to pick it up, and Nellie naturally halted that she might not walk over it.

On catching sight of the face of the man who had dropped the glove, Nellie instantly felt convinced that this was an accident done on purpose, and for the moment she felt very uncomfortable in being brought into such close quarters with the man whom, of all others in Rhyl, she hated.

As he stooped, she thought of instantly turning back and walking hurriedly away, but he was too quick for her.

" I really beg your pardon, madam."

" Not at all," replied Nellie, walking on.

The pretty widow was so quick in her movements that the solicitor was rather confounded, and suddenly forgot his set speech.

" I—I—I think I had the pleasure of—" Nellie increased her pace—" of playing with your little boys a day or two ago : fine little fellows."

Nellie bowed, and put more steam on.

" Pardon me, madam, had I not the pleasure of meeting you at the vicarage last Tuesday, at an evening party ?"

" I have never been there."

" It was my mistake. Lady Forton and her little boy were there, and I took her for yourself, and" —more steam—" what charming weather we are having."

" Excuse me, I do not wish to continue the conversation."

Poor Nellie was feeling very uncomfortable. There was not a creature to be seen the whole length of the East Parade, a most unusual circumstance, nor could Nellie see any one in any window she passed.

The solicitor saw the game was nearly up ; but at the same time, that the prize was worth a good struggle.

He argued that, as a widow, it was the duty of his idol to be very reserved, and backward in coming forward ; the more obstinate the fight the greater the ovation in the event of a triumph ;

the greater the modesty, bashfulness, &c., the stronger the love when the widowish, natural scruples had been overcome. So he argued.

"I beg your pardon," he again said, "I thought——"

"Be so good as not to walk with me."

"You are mistaken, I assure you, if you think that I have any motive but that of courtesy in addressing you."

"Courtesy! but again I beg you will leave me."

Had there been a single creature near, Nellie would have almost thrown herself into his or her arms. She could see no one, however.

But some one appeared.

The solicitor began to address her again at the very moment that Nellie and himself arrived immediately under the window of him whom we have hitherto called the quiet admirer.

Nellie stopped and looked him straight in the face.

"Will you instantly leave me?"

The solicitor parried the direct thrust with what he thought a very softening sentence.

"Do not let me offend you, my dear madam. I had hoped——"

"Again, I beg you to leave me, and instantly."

"Really, madam, I——"

The quiet admirer, who had been sitting at his window, had heard quite enough to justify him in vaulting from the room over the railings on to the *trottoir*.

One second after he had alighted—and he came down with a most sonorous drop—his knuckles were running into the back of the solicitor's neck.

"Now if you don't leave this lady alone, I'll give you a thundering good hiding."

"What the——"

"Now mizzle, or I'll be as good as my word.

Yes, I will. Now show your discretion by taking yourself off, and by Jove, if I catch you speaking to her again, you vulgar brute, I'll half kill you."

The quiet admirer, as we are aware, was somewhat Herculean, and the solicitor, too, was no little man, but the latter was no match for the gentleman whose knuckles had been running into him.

The solicitor made an impudent reply, whereupon the quiet admirer raised his powerful weighty fist, and——

"Pray don't, pray don't," pleaded Nellie.

And he *don'ted,* as poor Artemus would have said.

The lawyer moved off saying his say, of which, however, the quiet admirer took no notice.

"Take my arm, Mrs. Lorford, you are a little upset by that vagabond; come into this house where my mother and I are staying, and sit down for a minute or two."

Leaning on the arm of her deliverer, Nellie walked up the steps and went into the room in which the quiet admirer had been sitting.

"I will ring for my mother's maid, Mrs. Lorford."

"Pray don't, Sir Harry, pray don't; I am simply a little flurried. I shall be quite comfortable in one minute."

How little did Nellie expect to see her old lover in Rhyl! What recollections crowded and elbowed one another in her mind as she sat before him!

He had the advantage of her.

He had seen her fifty times, but he had kept his secret very close; he had not told Lady Frankwell even.

He had wondered, as he got up each morning, whether some good fortune would bring him unobtrusively into her presence, and as day passed day, he began to fear that fate meant to be unkind.

He had never dared to go up and address her, and he felt so jealous of his secret that he delayed day after day telling his mother, wishing to be himself the first to speak to the pretty widow.

He had made up his mind within the last few days that at the beginning of the following week he would tell his mother of Nellie's presence in Rhyl, and ask her to call. The events of this morning, however, hastened matters.

Now Nellie had very sincere regard for Sir Harry, for she thought that he had been very badly used; he had been led into supposing that she loved him, and he had consequently made love to and proposed to her, and after having been accepted—with what pain he could not guess—he had been eloped from.

Her regard was heightened from the fact of Archibald Lorford thinking so well of him, talking of him a hundred times admiringly and sympathetically at Allansay, and she held that he had behaved most good-naturedly after the elopement, and that independently of that, he deserved very high consideration from the manner in which he had behaved to her family.

Sir Harry, therefore, was no ordinary friend in Nellie's eyes; he was a friend with whom she could indulge in one of those conversations which are as chloroform to a troubled mind. First grief had spent its first force, and there was now no pleasure greater than in speaking of him who was gone to one who had known him, to one whose friendship was most honest and true. And Nellie felt no embarrassment in the presence of the man from whom she had once eloped.

After kind inquiries about Lady Frankwell, whom Nellie really loved, whom she was most anxious to

see, that she might open her heart and take comfort she said, "A great deal has happened, Sir
Harry, since I last saw you."

The young M.P was silent.

He was not a man at all for an embarrassing
situation. He was under the impression that
Nellie would not allude to painful subjects at all,
and he felt quite unable to speak to her opening
remark.

Nellie sat upon the sofa, her worthy good-hearted
Herculean deliverer hardly knowing where to put
himself, what to do, what to say.

Nellie came to his relief, and though she continued to speak upon the painful subject, very soon
convinced him that she took comforting pleasure
in the nature of the conversation, and that his
company was a source of cheerfulness to her.

It was great pleasure to Nellie to open her heart
to Sir Harry, and he immensely enjoyed this display of real friendship, after he had got over the
nervousness caused by the idea that she might, any
moment, burst into tears.

Such a display of trouble would unnerve him,
and just at first he dreaded it.

Nellie talked about Archibald Lorford for half
an hour, and in no doleful manner, so that Sir
Harry felt pleasantly at ease, and administered
much to Nellie's comfort by his kind, considerate,
and thoughtful remarks.

She picked up spirits wonderfully, and allowed a
smile or two occasionally to brighten her lovely
face.

This was almost the first conversation of the
kind Nellie had had since her husband's death.
The widow *mère* had touched upon the subject
months ago, intending to be sympathetic, and
meaning to give her sorrowing daughter an oppor-

tunity of letting loose some of the feelings of her over-full heart, but the widow *fille* had discouraged her.

Subsequently Nellie had talked on the subject with her banker uncle, and also with a cousin, but not with half the solace she felt now in Sir Harry's presence.

It was Lady Frankwell, however, whom Nellie was above all things longing to see. She loved the old lady, had loved her all her life, and had received a thousand kindnesses from her before and during the unhappy love-making in Cavendish Square. Nellie knew that the old lady was as much to be pitied as Sir Harry, and she now longed to nestle in her motherliness, and draw love and consolation from her.

"Have you seen my boys, Sir Harry?"

"Aye, that I have, Mrs. Lorford, and I may say that I dined off one of them the other day."

Nellie smiled.

"It is a fact, indeed. I was walking along the shore, when suddenly I heard a sound as of a little child crying, and looking round I saw young Master Lorford."

"How did you know it was he? have you seen me before to-day, Sir Harry?"

"I have, indeed, Mrs. Lorford, fifty times, and I somehow or other—somehow or other I couldn't, I——. I meant to tell my mother that you were in Rhyl, and then of course she would have called upon you, as she will do now with the greatest pleasure, and—and, yes, I saw your little boy, and very soon discovered that he had lost his nurse. I found the young lady presently talking to two medical students, a pair of impudent rascals, and had the misfortune to box the ears of one of them rather severely. I sat for a few minutes on the

steps of a bathing machine, put your little fellow
on my knee, gave him my watch to play with, and
had a brief conversation with him about—about
you, and after kissing him a dozen times—I never
kissed a child in my life before, Mrs. Lorford—
I took him back to his nurse and gave her a little
good advice. Upon my word, I may say, I dined
off him, for, to my mother's astonishment, I scarcely
touched an atom at dinner that day."

Nellie felt as if she could have talked for hours,
it was such relief to her to talk. And she could
see no impropriety whatever, as a widow, in talking
to a gentleman from whom she had had the misfortune to elope some three years ago.

Sooner than she would have actually liked, however, she felt it best to get up to leave.

" My protecting arm is at your service, Mrs.
Lorford."

" Well, Sir Harry, if you will be so kind as to
escort me home I shall be glad, as it is just
possible that my disturber may be loitering about."

And of course the young M.P walked home
with the pretty widow.

Lady Frankwell had not returned when the two
set out, but Sir Harry promised to bring her to
Church Street in the course of the day.

He hoped that Nellie would ask him to come in
now for a minute or two, and she herself was
wondering at the same moment if she could very
well make such a request.

They reached the door, and just as Sir Harry
held out his hand for a shake, he felt his tongue
wag, and heard himself say, " Well, Mrs. Lorford,
will you let me see your boys for half a minute?"

" Certainly, Sir Harry, if you'll promise not to
dine off them !"

He promised, and within two minutes he had

both boys upon his lap, and he pleased Nellie as much as he surprised her with the amusing command he possessed over infantile language.

The half minute gone, or rather the quarter of an hour to which it was prolonged, Sir Harry left Nellie and her offspring, and walked homewards.

His were strange sensations now, stranger perhaps than he had ever before experienced under any circumstances whatever.

He was in a state of lulled excitement. Excitement was natural to him; it was his element, almost his food. For nearly two years now he had lived to a great extent upon the ever-engrossing excitement of the House; upon close divisions, rumours of resignations, and the like, upon defeats and victories, and now the crowning excitement had fallen upon him, but it came as a sedative.

There was something about Nellie, in herself and in her history, which lulled while it excited him; she was an object of intense fascination, enveloped in a kind of sanctity by reason of her widowhood.

A hundred looks to-day put him in mind of a hundred looks that had fascinated him during the Cavendish Square love-making; one or two of Nellie's own peculiar expressions revived in him a recollection of very happy days in the W postal district, and really once or twice Sir Harry all but forgot what he was saying, so lost was he in thought and recollections.

Was there any difference between Nellie Branston and Nellie Lorford?

A great difference, the more adorable angel being decidedly Nellie Lorford.

Nellie Branston was lovely, Nellie Lorford magnificent. Miss Branston angelic, Mrs. Lorford archangelic. Nellie Branston was a darling to be petted and cherished, Nellie Lorford a woman to be adored and honoured.   Sir Harry settled all this in a second, and he found no difficulty in coming to this opinion upon the present adorableness of the archangel he had just left.

For the life of him, however, he could not imagine what Nellie Lorford, *widow*, might think of Harry Frankwell, *bachelor !*

And he could not solve the difficulty either by Euclid or algebra.

No.   But only fancy, my reader, if such a solution were practicable, to what a nicety would not wranglers and optimes, seniores and juniores, determine the probabilities of their winning the affections of the Ameliæ, Selinæ, and Jemimæ of the world !   Even the 'wooden spoon' might put down his Louisa as x, and work her out *à la* simple equation, in a manner that could leave no doubt as to whether he would win or lose !

As for Euclid, it is to be feared that the immortal *pons* of the first book would bridge over none of love's difficulties, even for the greatest of asses ! And by what other proposition would any one think of working love ?   Time alone could solve the equation for Sir Harry, and oh ! what a long process is this too often ; how many hours, months, aye, and sometimes years have to be rubbed out before the equivalent to that wretched little x is found, before the answer comes out in its delightful unmistakableness !

Two years and the House of Commons had done a great deal for Sir Harry Frankwell—so Nellie thought.

Good looking she always pronounced him, but she also had thought him very fast and slang, and excruciatingly Bond Street in dress.

When he went out of doors three years ago he never seemed to Nellie simply to leave the house, but always to be turned out of it as if from a mould. He walked too in a stiff, mould-like manner, whenever he set out to do the Park or stare into the Ride; he prided himself on being natural *per se,* but to Nellie he looked anything but natural on being turned out of the mould.

Swells never dress well; they dress smartly and nothing more, and to do this they take one page out of the book of snobbery, and several out of that of foppery. The agony their exquisite smartness causes them could hardly be exceeded by what would result from the extraction of a tooth: the former, however, being somewhat of a lingering death; they look like so much Tunbridge ware, and you fancy that if you were to take out a pin or stud they would fall to pieces!

The House of Commons had taught Sir Harry how to dress; he now dressed absolutely well, expensively and well. Formerly he had dressed expensively and badly, too nearly *à la* swell. The House too had rubbed off a good deal of the slang and by Jove-ing, but, as was inevitable, it had taught him some of its own slang.

The appearance he now presented to Nellie was one of vast improvement. Being country-bred, she had a natural aversion to excruciating swellery, and she had a good eye for taste in male attire, having had so faultless a model as Archibald Lorford.

Nellie had noticed, and indeed could not have failed to notice, Sir Harry's superior style; and without doing violence to her feelings in the matter of one ever to be loved and never to be forgotten, she confessed that Sir Harry remodelled was a fine-looking, fascinating, engaging fellow.

She did not regret having asked him in to see the boys; and she did not regret the solicitorial im-

pudence which had called forth his gallant inter-
ference.

On the whole, she entertained no unfavourable
opinion of Harry Frankwell, *bachelor*. And she,
be it remembered, was Nellie Lorford, *widow*.

Boys will be boys, young men will be young
men, and—young widows will be young widows!
And why should they not? Are they hard-hearted
in being simply natural? I trow not.

Nellie was a girl of the highest Toryism in the
matter of affections, and possessed the tenderest of
hearts; those of my readers, therefore, who may
have been jumping at conclusions in consequence
of the foregoing remarks, had better jump back.

If they must jump at all, let them wait till they
have read one or two more chapters. Young
widows, however, will be young widows, and quite
right too!

The solicitor went home discomfited; the pretty
widow was not for him. With this Herculean fellow in the place—a fellow with a head that was not
to be punched—there was no use trying luck again;
he could not do better than go. To stay would
probably be to see the rival more than ever trium-
phant; that would be a sight unpleasant, for
hitherto the solicitor had made many conquests,
and knuckles in the back of his neck produced a
sensation entirely new to him. He could not do
better than go.

> Me wretched! Let me curr to quercine shades!
> Effund your albid hausts, lactif'rous maids!
> Oh! might I vole to some umbrageous clump,
> Depart—be off—excede—evade—erump!

CHAPTER XIII.

CAPTAIN FRANKWELL IN LOVE.

LADY FRANKWELL, like Nellie Lorford, had come to Rhyl to bathe her boy; and I may add that her son took to the water rather more kindly than Master Lorford.

Twenty-four hours before the occurrence of events just related, Lady Frankwell had for the first time spied Nellie on the Parade, and she instantly thought that a removal to Llandudno would be for the harmonious advantage of her son.

She told Sir Harry of her discovery, and of course he would not hear of the removal; but he begged her not to call on Nellie just yet, hoping, for one thing, that he might meet her himself, or that his mother might accidentally stumble across her in the course of a few days.

In consideration, however, of the interview that had just taken place, Sir Harry begged her ladyship to call at once.

"She is looking splendid, mother, absolutely gorgeous, and I am frightfully in love with her. She has grown and developed into a superb woman; there is not another in the kingdom that can touch her; I am at her feet; I am literally enslaved; she is a Tritoness, I am a minnow."

"Well, Harry, I wish with all my heart that we had not happened to meet her."

"Why, best of mothers? why?"

"Because you instantly re-fall in love with her,

get violently excited, and buoy yourself up with
the idea that there is some chance now of her falling in love with you. You have not actually said
so, but I am not far wrong in my supposition;
now, am I, Harry?"

"My dear mother, I have re-fallen in love with
Nellie; there is no doubt about that; what will
follow is yet buried in the tomb of uncertainty."

"Harry, dear, Mrs. Lorford has been a widow
barely two years, and, judging by the intensity of
her affection for her late husband, and knowing
her character as well as I do, I should say she would
never marry again."

"Nonsense, mother; widows will be widows!
You know what I mean."

"Scandalous fellow, you mean just the opposite
to what you say. Well, Harry, if you say anything to Mrs. Lorford in the least degree approaching love for at least a whole year, you'll——"

"Be a fool, and give fresh proofs of the sad
emptiness of the head! Perhaps so, dear mother,
perhaps not. Nothing venture, nothing win."

"Yes, Harry, and nothing hazard, nothing lose.
And I don't think you can afford to hazard your
affections a second time."

"We will adjourn the discussion; and in the
meantime, do you put on your coal-scuttle bonnet,
and otherwise get ready to be escorted to Church
Street."

Sir Harry left his mother at Nellie's lodgings,
promising to call for her in half an hour's time.

Her ladyship was a warm-hearted old lady, and
felt sure that Nellie would feel pleased with a little
display of affection on first meeting; so she kissed
the pretty widow right heartily, and met with an
equally affectionate response.

L

How women do kiss, to be sure! And why should they not? Better do that than nothing!

Like a pair of thorough-going women, Lady Frankwell and Nellie betrayed tears on the conclusion of the kissing.

We can guess every word they said during this interview; we can guess, to some extent, the greatness of the pleasure Nellie felt in telling the old lady a hundred matters connected with her terrible troubles.

The boys were discussed—not Nellie's only, but Lady Frankwell's too, and the Herculean deliverer got anything but abuse.

Sir Harry fetched his mother in due course, and of necessity Nellie made him come in, and of necessity he talked to her very pleasantly, and played with the handsome boys.

Lady Frankwell had nothing of importance to tell her son respecting the interview, but on the next visit she elicited something which she deemed it right Sir Harry should at once be told.

During this call, she worked Nellie round to a certain point upon which she was a little anxious to have positive information. Her ladyship asked no direct questions—that would have been indelicate—but she elicited this reply from the pretty widow—"I really am in no hurry to fix upon a home, Lady Frankwell, for I shall never marry again; I prefer travelling about quietly, and really think that constant change does the boys good."

This reply was communicated to Sir Harry, great stress being laid upon the words 'for I shall never marry again.'

Sir Harry listened and smiled.

"Bless your heart, my wonderful mother, I never feel more proud of you than when you give me

proof that you are not what is called a woman of
the world. You have told me Nellie's reply with
most exquisite simplicity; alas! that I should be
such a ruffian as to receive it with most uncom-
promising worldliness, with a whole mine of salt,
in fact. It is not unfeeling to say that young
widows of about two years' standing *do* think of
marrying again; and when the widow meets with
an old lover, still a bachelor, it is seldom that she
is proof against his charms, let them be never so
slight in the eyes of the general world. Mother,
dear, I adore Nellie with most fearful adoration,
and I swear that if I don't marry her, that I'll not
marry at all, and Dudsworth and Ledgington may
go to the Frankwells of nowhere as soon as Gil
has done with them. But I must marry Nellie,
and before many months too. I shall not go to
Scotland; the grouse may go to the devil; I shall
stay here and make love."

"My dear Harry, Fenella means what she
says——"

"She's a wonderful widow then!"

"She does indeed: then you will be refused,
and what will happen next? Why——"

"I shall persevere; I shall dun her, mother, I
shall dun her, and then I must win. You never
knew a dun beaten, did you?"

"I never have had any experience with duns,
and have no wish that way. Well, Harry, you
must do as you like, of course; and if you are
refused, you'll be laid up, and though you will have
me and plenty of doctors to nurse you, you'll find
that not one of us will be able to minister to a
mind diseased."

"Most apt quotation, dear mother, and one to
which I cannot do better than reply in the words

of Macbeth's family physician himself—'Therein
the patient must minister to himself.' That's just
what I should have said myself, and have thought
my guinea well earned. I'll write my own pre·
scriptions, and depend upon it I shall want no
'sweet oblivious antidote,' after all, for I mean to
win. And now, dear Lady Macbeth, you must
cease your funning for awhile, as I intend to write
home for the drag and bays. By Jove, I mean to
make love in style, as a Tory M.P. ought."

In a very short space of time the immortal drag
arrived, and with it Lieutenant and Captain Gilbert
Howden Frankwell, of the Guards.

A drag in Rhyl was an event, and if it had no
other very remarkable effect it had this one—it
made the London solicitor see that he had rather
higher game to contend with than he had imagined.
He dropped the pretty widow even in thought; he had
once hoped that this stalwart owner of the sharp
knuckles would move away, and leave the coast
clear; now, however, he saw the emptiness of the
hope, and resolved to move away himself.

Captain Frankwell had never seen Nellie. He
was in Canada during Sir Harry's love-making,
and, since the elopement, had of course enjoyed no
opportunity of getting sight of the beauty. He
had not seen her twice in Rhyl, however, before he
was led to thump his fist upon his knee and say,
"The only girl this world possesses about whom I
could care sixpence."

Love at first sight.

Do you deny the possibility of heart-photography
by the instantaneous process?

I trow not.

Gilbert Frankwell, to whom I must devote a few
lines, was one of the quietest Guardsmen alive,

one who, wondrous fact, almost thought too little
of himself. He was an amazingly good-looking
fellow, an inch shorter than his brother : that is to
say, about five feet ten, but far handsomer. Sir
Harry had a pleasing, fascinating face, with the
manly attraction of good beard and whiskers.
Gilbert was thoroughly handsome, a full-bodied
moustache, the perfection of shape, his sole facial
attraction in a hirsute way.

Sir Harry was light, Gilbert dark.

The Guardsman was better built, better strung
together, than the M.P. He was equally massive
and muscular, but more dapper and smart. Large,
black, expressive, brilliant eyes he had, which
could pierce the pretty sex through and through.

Gilbert was a quiet fellow, but by no means slow,
and he liked to be left as much as possible to himself. Everything he had was of the best; there
was nothing in his possession which modern vul-
garity would not call "first-class." If he had not
the best T cart and pair of horses in the brigade,
no man had better. His quarters were unique in
the matter of furniture and general adornments.
He, lucky fellow, had always plenty of ready
money; always a really fine cigar for friends, and
by no means "second-class" ones for acquaint-
ances even. There was no man in the best dressed
brigade in the army better dressed than he; no
man more quiet, more undemonstrative, less fast,
less wild. Gilbert was universally liked, and the
Colonel, more than once, had privately held him up
as his idea of a Guardsman.

The loudest men liked him, but not more than
the few quiet ones, for Gilbert was no drone ; he
could go neck and neck with the best in turn out,
conversation, fun, style, and in all matters that had

any go in them of any laudable description. Nine-tenths he could out-pace in the matter of money; although he went the pace, he knew when to put the drag on.

All his life, his military life especially, he had avoided running after beauty; and he had studi-ously avoided, so far as he was able, leading any one to regard him as a catch. He hated the idea.

Now, Nellie had taken his fancy immensely. She knew nothing of Guards'-worship, a species of idolatry Gilbert knew to be universal in metropo-litan regions. She was no idolatress, but ap-parently a most comely, unaffected, unsophisticated English girl, one who looked far more like a bride than a widow. There was a matronliness, however, about her in which Gilbert saw dignity and great fascination, and he was smitten, rather deeply too.

Not a day passed now on which Nellie and the Frankwells did not meet, and Sir Harry was bury-ing himself in love. One day, after a good deal of persuasion, which brought out Nellie's modesty of widowhood very charmingly, she consented to mount the immortal drag. This was proof positive to Sir Harry that if she were not actually forgetting her troubles, she was willing to mend her broken heart by what he thought the best remedy, namely gentle diversion.

Fearfully in love though he was, there were times when Sir Harry felt that there might be something in what his mother had said of the folly of making downright love yet awhile. He would hover about as long as he could, always dancing attendance upon opportunity.

All this time Captain Frankwell was being smitten, and he was making himself very agreeable to Nellie. Gilbert had the knack of doing the agreeable to perfection, a knack of which he was well aware ; one too of which he made use but very sparingly in the company of unsophisticated beauties, for fear of misleading to even the most homœopathic extent.

The eyes of Lady Frankwell had been kept rather widely open of late, and what she had seen had a little perplexed her. She fancied she had seen enough to justify a new belief that Nellie might possibly listen to Sir Harry's love advances in the course of a year or so, and she fancied too that Gilbert was fully aware that his brother was in love, resolved to win if possible.

Now Gilbert had no positive idea that Sir Harry had an eye to Nellie's heart, and this gradually dawned upon his mother, replacing her previous idea, and, therefore, perplexing her.

Suppose it were really a fact that her two sons were irrecoverably in love with Nellie.

What was the poor mother to do ?

What were Sir Harry's ideas ?

Why, he had no idea whatever that Gilbert was not right well aware that he, the old lover, had loving designs upon the pretty widow.

And what thought Gilbert ?

Why, he was of opinion that Nellie was not very likely to fall in love with the very man from whom a few years ago she had positively eloped.

Gilbert was a very quiet, reticent fellow, and therefore I cannot pretend to dive deeply into his mind. As events happened, so shall they be recorded.

Lady Frankwell hesitated to interfere in any way between the brothers, though she daily feared a fratricidal war of the heart. She, however, only

bided her time : the iron was in the fire gradually
reddening ; when hot, she would strike.

There was no occasion, however, for her ladyship to trouble herself, as Sir Harry found it necessary to take matters into his own hands.

It was now nine weeks since Sir Harry had delivered Nellie out of the hands of the discomfited
solicitor, and not one day had passed, during that
time, on which deliverer and delivered had not met.
Surely, Sir Harry thought, it could not be too soon
to.propose, or too soon, at all events, to ascertain,
somewhat clearly, how Nellie's affections lay.

Of course the pretty widow had given just one or
two little thoughts about love, to ascertain her own
feelings *in re* marrying again, and it did not take
her long to settle in what way she would best consult her own happiness. Sir Harry was burning to
tell his love, and make sure of Nellie once and for
all. He could hardly take his eyes off her for a
second, each day, during a visit, drive, or quiet
dinner. He slept very little for thinking of her ;
he ate very little, because he lived so much upon
her beauty and fascinations, and he talked very little
because he had almost lost the gift of speech
through the eloquent silence of stupendous admiration.

Nellie was one of those women of whom Gilbert
had occasionally read ; he had never actually seen
anyone in the slightest degree approaching her ex-
cellence. Gilbert looked upon her as a marvellous
woman, because she could subdue, rule, fascinate,
confound, enslave, bewilder, and inexpressibly
charm him. She was a glorious woman, the exception, not the rule of the sex : a woman of brains
and understanding, of devotion, and pure feminine
gentleness ; no dangerous tactician, no mere orderer

of dinner, and receiver of company, no tract-reading, timid, common-place, ill-educated, animate mummy; but a perfect companion for a man, for one like himself, manly in mind and body.

Hitherto he had been no woman-worshipper; he had thought her such a poor thing to worship, such an uncompanionable thing, though, altogether, something unrivalled for playing with, petting, and teasing.

But Nellie was in his eyes a real WOMAN, the genuine creation as designed originally, B.C. 4004.

With all her rustic simplicity, Nellie was most polished and well-bred, accomplished, and keenly sensible, and with her present perfections of mind and manner, Archibald Lorford had had much to do.

Nellie had great natural talents, which would have been more fully developed had she been more under the influence of her father, one of those old courtier-like, well-educated, well-born rectors, of whom 1867 boasts too few. Two years in the constant society of such a man as her late husband, and two years' absence from her very commonplace mother, had worked wonders for her, and she was now in every particular the woman that Captain Frankwell believed her.

That Gilbert loved her beyond expression, there could be little doubt; but whether he would allow his love to take its natural course, or whether he would smother it, if able, on seeing the bent of his brother's affections, was another matter altogether.

All this must be shown by the record of coming events.

Gilbert discovered Sir Harry's love, but not so soon as might have been expected, because he thought it so utterly unlikely that Nellie would give the man she had run away from a thought even in widowhood.

Gilbert admitted, however, that love might have blinded his own eyes.

All this while Lady Frankwell's state of mind was not comfortable ; as I have before said, she was dreading a fratricidal war of the heart.

She found no opportunity for interfering however ; neither son said a word to her, and indeed it was not likely that the elder would dream of saying a word, because he was so fully under the impression that Gilbert knew which way the wind blew.

To suggest that Nellie was anybody's widow but Sir Harry's, would have been looked upon as an indication of lunacy by our worthy Parliamentary friend.

Sir Harry took the matter into his own hands, purposely avoiding saying a word to his good mother.

In fact, he wanted to sail round her. Her ladyship said, " It is too soon to propose." Sir Harry said, " I don't think it is, and I want to show your ladyship that I am right."

So he took the matter into his own hands, keeping his own counsel as Gilbert kept his, and with what result we shall presently discover.

CHAPTER XIV

NOTHING HAZARD, NOTHING LOSE.

ONE afternoon, Lady Frankwell and Gilbert went to call at the vicarage, leaving Sir Harry upon the sofa to nurse a headache.

Our worthy friend had been by no means well for the last ten days. His excitable temperament often got him into trouble inducing great nervousness, and if he did not happen to be quite the thing at the time, it caused a general upset. His was not a strong constitution at the present time, though naturally of an adamantine nature, and the nervous headache from which he was now suffering was a gentle reminder that he had two or three screws about him which could hardly be considered tight, and that one of them was most decidedly loose now.

"Oh! hang the headache," he said, a few minutes after Lady Frankwell and Gilbert had left, "I'll go and see Nellie's boys."

He had bought a present for the little fellows a day or two ago, and he would take it this afternoon as a sort of excuse for visiting Church Street.

Douglas usually managed to descry him coming along the road, as the little man's favourite place in the room was on a stool by the bow-window. Seeing Sir Harry this afternoon, he ran out to meet him, *non invitâ* Mary, and escorted him into the sitting-room.

"Mamma gone out," he said.

Sir Harry 'hung it' internally, but taking a boy on each knee, prepared to make himself as happy as untoward circumstances would allow.

Nellie came in in less than a quarter of an hour, and oh! how Sir Harry's heart beat as he descried the lovely widow!

"I just ran in, Mrs. Lorford, to see if I could get rid of a tiresome, undeserved headache by playing with your boys, and behold, in ten minutes they have cured me."

"Well, Sir Harry, I am very glad to hear of the cure; and as you have made use of my boys, I shall make use of you. Run out of the room, little ones; I can't have any chatter while I ask Sir Harry Frankwell's advice about a matter which mamma is not quite clever enough to understand. Now, Sir Harry, you will save me the trouble of going to the bank, or possibly to a lawyer, if you will read this letter, and tell me why my income is less this quarter by nine pounds than it ever has been."

Sir Harry knew as much about law and business as his drag.

He drew a chair to the table, looked amazingly wise, like the sham clerk in the farce of a *Fish out of Water*, and spread out the letter before him. But he did not read it. He could not; he got through the first two lines and then forgot what they were about, and so failed to make the slightest sense out of the third.

"Have you read it?" asked Nellie.

"No, not yet."

"Well, Sir Harry, I'm afraid you never will read it if you keep looking at me."

"Very true ; so you must not stand just before me, or I shall be sure to look at you."

This was pretty plain.

Nellie was taking off her hat whilst she was standing before her lover, and he was watching her. She was warm with walking, and her cheeks were literally *couleur de rose*, and her eyes the nearest approach to blue diamonds this world ever saw.

Nellie now seated herself on the sofa behind her adviser, and her heart beat a little fast after the above conversation.

Sir Harry read and re-read the letter, and could get neither rhyme nor reason out of it, and between every three or four lines he took a look at Nellie.

When he had gone over it for the third time, he began to talk very earnestly about it, and wound up by saying that he would consult a friend of his in Rhyl, a barrister.

A greengrocer could have solved the difficulty, or a Welsh juryman, which is saying a great deal. Nellie's want of experience in matters concerning interest, consols, dividends, and the like, alone prevented her thoroughly understanding why her income was a little less this quarter than usual. She had guessed, and was quite right too in her guess, and she only wanted some one to put the same construction upon the matter as herself to assure her of her own correctness.

It began to dawn upon her that Sir Harry was no business man, and she hoped to extract a little fun out of the fact.

"I have no doubt you understand so trivial a

matter yourself, Sir Harry, but find a difficulty in explaining it clearly and simply to a poor member of the unbusiness-like sex."

Now Sir Harry was at all times anxious to appear before Nellie in the most favourable light possible, and two or three times he had felt a little extinguished in her presence by his sharp brother Gilbert. He knew perfectly well that Gil would be able to smooth the way in a second, and he feared greatly that Nellie might show him the letter, and thereby put another extinguisher indirectly upon the less brilliant brother. Yet Sir Harry was too honest to escape by the loop-hole Nellie had made.

"It is very good of you to say that to enable a clumsy, thick-headed fellow to get out of a difficulty which, I have no doubt, is no difficulty at all. 'Pon my word, however, Mrs. Lorford, I can see nothing in this letter to justify the bank in detaining nine pounds of your money. It doesn't look well, I confess, and the Bank of England, too —it's that which fogs me, for if it had been a bank of a fishy description, I should say at once the directors or the chairman, or somebody, was trying to do you. But the Bank of England"—he moved off his chair and seated himself on the sofa by Nellie—"I—I—oh! bother the nine pounds, I say; they're not worth a stamp for a letter to——"

"Well, you're a nice adviser, I must say, Sir Harry," said Nellie, laughing.

That little laugh, and the lovely bright look it brought into Nellie's sweet face upset the adviser in a second.

"Oh! my conscience, you'll be the death of me," he exclaimed, with passionate earnestness.

" Dear me, Sir Harry, what's the matter ?"

He seemed aware of the sudden display of incontrollable enthusiasm which he had manifested, and for a moment felt confused and embarrassed.

Nellie, too, was not perfectly at her ease.

" What did I say ?"

" Well, you charged me with possible murder," answered Nellie, trying to laugh off the embarrassment.

" Did I ? But—but—oh ! what's the use of attempting to conceal my feelings. Nellie, darling, I love you—I love you above all and everything. Oh ! Nellie, dearest, do let me keep this little hand, and do tell me that you love me."

Nellie's first answer was a flood of tears. This proposal was utterly unexpected, and its suddenness unnerved her.

" Oh ! my angel, my angel," cried Sir Harry, as he saw the tears flow, kissing poor Nellie with intense fervour and drawing her to him; " oh ! my angel, my angel."

" No, no, Sir Harry ; please loose my hand."

" My darling, darling Nellie," he continued, hearing not a word of the pretty widow's request in his enthusiastic excitement; " oh, Nellie, if you did but know how——"

" Oh ! Sir Harry, I pray you do not talk to me more in this way."

" Nellie, I worship you," and the great fellow sank upon his knees and kissed the hand of his goddess again and again. " Darling Nellie, you love me, you love me ; oh ! say you do. I will not get up till you tell me—till you make me the happiest fellow out of Heaven."

" I cannot tell you that I love you."

" Why, Nellie, why ?"

Nellie was silent. She could not plumply tell the poor pleading lover that she did not love him, and yet she was dying to say something which would have the effect of bringing him upon his legs, in which position she felt she could better cope with him than in his present supplicating attitude. She wanted to tell him the old, old story of liking as a friend and nothing more.

But he would not get up.

" Nellie, you cannot refuse me," he said.

" I can, Sir Harry, and I must."

" No, no, no—impossible, impossible ! Such love as mine cannot be thrown away : it is fixed upon you, Nellie, surely and firmly, and I only wish to live that I may love you. Oh, Nellie, darling, dry those tears ; do not try to take this hand away, but smile a little love, whisper a little love, look a little love."

Neither spoke for fully a minute, Nellie hanging down her head and weeping, Sir Harry holding her hand to his lips, and kissing it most fervently.

He got up and sat beside the tearful beauty. " Come, dearest Nellie, you know how madly I adore you ; you know what a perfect slave love has made me ; you know how immensely happy you can make me if you will but give me this little hand for life. You cannot refuse me ; no, no, why should you ?"

" If you love me, Sir Harry, you will say no more to me on this subject. I cannot love you, I can still less marry you."

This staggered the poor pleader ; he knew not what to reply. He thought Nellie was bound to love him, or rather that she did love him, for to him there appeared no earthly reason why she should not.

He could not believe that she meant what she said. "You are a naughty girl, tantalising me in this way, because you know that you mean to say 'yes' after you have driven me sufficiently mad with a 'no' or two, sufficiently to show that I love you too well to be refused." And the earnest expression of his face resolved itself into a smile. He felt happy because he felt convinced that Nellie was only plaguing him.

But she had to come down upon him with a few words, beside which the force of a steam-hammer would seem as nothing.

She rose to leave the room.

"I must leave you, Sir Harry; I cannot stay to hear you talk in this way. I hardly ever felt more unhappy in my—in my life. I——" And then the tears burst forth anew, and sobs rendered inaudible the rest of the sentence.

It is not in man to resist the appeal of feminine tears, but how was Sir Harry to yield? How could he show his subjection, his powerlessness? He spoke very quietly, his whole face showing the depth of his sympathy, as likewise the intensity of misery he felt at the prospect of losing one he loved with such boundless devotion.

"If you wish to leave, Nellie dearest, it would be most unkind, most unfeeling of me to try to prevent you, but seeing how I love you, you must see that to leave me would be to break my heart."

He paused a moment, and looked intently and imploringly into Nellie's face. She was trying very hard to stay her tears.

"I know you don't wish to break my heart, but

M

most assuredly you will break it if you tell me that you do not, that you can not, love me. Could anybody in this world love you more dearly than I ? No, Nellie ; and I am sure you must believe me when I say so. It is useless my trying to say how much I love you, because it is impossible that you could fail to tell the intensity of my affection. Could not I make you very happy, Nellie, if I married you? I think nothing about your deriving happiness from what it would be in my power to give you, because you are worth in yourself fifty such worlds as this, but could not my love make you happy? Oh ! Nellie, my darling, my angel, do not leave me, do not refuse me. It is not a mere form of words when I say that I cannot live without you ; it is perfect truth, Nellie ; you are more than half my life, and the loss of you would be the breaking of my heart, and in fact my death."

" It almost kills me, indeed it does, to hear you talk in this way, for I know you love me, I know you would do anything for me ; yes, with all your heart."

" I would, Nellie."

" But I cannot marry you, I cannot, Sir Harry, indeed I cannot, and I pray you—I implore you— never ask me again. Oh, dear, dear, I feel so un-happy. I feel quite ill in having to say this to you."

" And how do you suppose that I feel in having to hear you say this? O Nellie, Nellie, I have built a thousand thoughts of unimaginable hap-piness upon the idea of winning your love. I have believed that there was a new life, a new world opening for me through you, and now where is the happiness I had thought of? Where is this new life to which every day spent in your company

has seemed to bring me nearer ?   Nellie, I implore
you be not so cruel as to refuse me.   Oh! do not
kill me, do not, do not——"

He could say no more; he burst into tears, the
violence of his emotion throwing him well nigh
into a fit.

Poor Nellie was alarmed, and what more natural
than that she should cry more bitterly than ever ?

"My darling, darling angel, do not cry, I pray
you; it breaks my heart to see you in this way,
Nellie. I will leave you; I am a wretch to make
you cry; I am a selfish, unmanly wretch, and I
will hurt you no more. O my poor, poor heart!"
Saying this he buried his face in his hands, a
moment after sinking upon his knees, and almost
falling upon the floor. He kissed Nellie's hand a
dozen times, and hurriedly rising up, hastened
from the room, distracted, and all but mad.

*   *   *   *
  *   *   *   *

These stars, my reader, mean a great deal, far
more, in fact, than I could accurately tell you word
by word, line by line. You must allow them to
help Sir Harry, the deliverer, the adviser, the bis-
rejected one, to his lodgings on the East Parade.
There Lady Frankwell and Gilbert found him on
their return. Sir Harry was walking up and down
the room in a most painfully excited state, crying
out at times, and wildly gesticulating.

"My dear, dear Harry," exclaimed his good
mother, not a little alarmed, though comparatively
used to his vagaries and eccentricities.

"This is all your doing, Gil, and a —— nice
brother *you* are," growled Sir Harry.

"Now sit still, Harry, and don't make such a

confounded row; sit still, and tell me what on
earth you mean by implying that I am the cause of
this diabolical noise and foolery."

"So you are."

"Now sit still and explain." And gently, though
determinedly, Gilbert forced his big brother on to
the sofa.

Then came out the why and wherefore.

Sir Harry felt convinced that Gilbert had been
trying to supplant him in Nellie's affections, and
that she had merely refused the elder brother
for the younger, not because she had no intention
of marrying again.

"She's in love with you, Gil."

"And if she is, is that a just reason for your
swearing at me? I don't know, however, that
Mrs. Lorford cares sixpence about me: she has
never given me cause to think so. Don't be so
fast with your condemnation, Harry."

"Well, you mustn't be hard upon me, Gil; a
fellow hardly knows what he is saying or doing
when he feels as much cut up as I. By Jove, Gil,
hanging isn't worse than being refused."

"Well, Harry, I've had no pleasant time, I can
assure you, since I saw that you were in love with
your old flame. She must be more than an ordinary
girl who can upset my equilibrium, but, as true as
eggs are eggs, Mrs. Lorford floored me at first sight.
I've done nothing out of the way to make myself
adorable in her eyes, that I am aware of: she'll
have you in time, Harry."

"And that will cut you up: but she won't have
me, she won't have me, she'll either never marry
again, or else she'll kill me by marrying some fellow
that isn't fit to black her boots."

Sir Harry was greatly upset, far more than when the reaction, after the elopement, set in.

His highly excitable temperament led him at times to a state of excitement which really verged upon madness, and such was the case now. Hardly had Gilbert left the room, after the above conversation, when Sir Harry got up from the sofa, and in a most frantic manner commenced walking, or rather tearing, up and down the room, gesticulating, swearing, and violently exciting himself. Gilbert, hearing the noise, instantly came back. Usually he could master his brother, but to-day he seemed almost powerless beside him, and Lady Frankwell, who was terribly frightened, seeing this, rang at once for the footman.

With this auxiliary force, Gilbert managed to get Sir Harry down upon the sofa, and there he kept him for half an hour.

He remained pretty quiet the rest of the evening, hardly indeed speaking, but working hard, as Lady Frankwell could see, to subdue emotions, whose only relief, she feared, could be in a fresh burst of excitement, or perhaps of bitter tears.

In tears Nellie Lorford had spent the hour succeeding Sir Harry's departure. She was sorry for the poor fellow from the depths of her warm and loving heart. He did love her, and most passionately too, she could see, and she felt for him acutely.

Once she had accepted, and run away from him: now she had emphatically rejected him.

Nellie's heart was powerfully moved when she thought of this, and in her quiet way she was every bit as much upset as Sir Harry.

Gilbert was glad that some kind of crisis had come.

He did admire Nellie to the full limit, as he fancied, of human admiration, but since he had discovered Sir Harry's weakness for her, he had tried hard not to let his admiration flower and become love. It had budded, however, despite all he could do, and now he hoped that a few weeks or days would let him see whether or not he must destroy the bud. He could not bring himself to attempt to cut out Sir Harry, but surely he would not be acting in an unbrotherly manner if he wooed Nellie after her distinct refusal to accept the earlier suitor?

He would bide his time, and refrain from influencing in any way the tide that must roll either to him or from him.

Lady Frankwell and Gilbert waited breakfast a quarter of an hour for Sir Harry the following morning. Gilbert then ran up and found his brother still in bed, his eyes bearing testimony to a tearful, sleepless night.

Did he not intend to get up?

No, he never meant to get up again.

"Nonsense, my dear Harry, if you get up, the good mater and I will cheer you, and——"

"No, Gil, this cruel refusal is killing me. I want to be quite alone, and I don't care if I die in an hour."

Sir Harry remained in bed the whole of that day and the next, and he hardly ate or drank more than would have sustained a kitten. He was constantly in tears, crying as Samsons only cry when Love's varied troubles try them.

On the third morning the M.P got up.

This morning Lady Frankwell resolved that she would no longer delay calling upon Nellie. She had

been thinking of so doing once or twice since the
great catastrophe, and had taken counsel with Gilbert. The committee had decided that it would be
better to wait until Sir Harry had come round a
little, and so the call was deferred. Her ladyship
would wait no longer, she would go to-day.

"I shall tell her she must marry Harry"

"My dear mother——"

"Leave her to me, Gilbert, I shall know what to
say to her when I see her. I can't allow her to put
my boy into fits."

So her ladyship set out to try and induce
Nellie Lorford, *widow,* to accept Harry Frankwell,
bachelor.

And Gilbert sat still to wonder whether it was
likely that her ladyship would be successful.

The front door of the house where Nellie lodged
was open, as also that of the sitting-room. So the
old lady walked in *sans cérémonie.* Much to her
ladyship's delight, Nellie was sitting alone, and in
one moment the pretty widow was in her arms kissing her fervently.

This looked well.

After a few preliminary words, Nellie said—

"Oh, Lady Frankwell, why did you not come and
see me before? I have been *so* unhappy."

"Well, my dear, you have thrown my poor boy
into fits, and I have had to look closely after him,
for this is the first day he has been up since
Tuesday."

"Dear Lady Frankwell, I am afraid you had
never told him what I stated to you, namely, that I
should not marry again."

"Oh yes, my dear, I told him that weeks ago,
and he would not allow himself to believe such a

thing; nor will I now. No, no, I won't, indeed. Now don't cry, but sit quietly down and talk to me sensibly. You know that I love you, and that I love Harry too, and I am also in hopes that some day *you* will love my poor Harry, for his love of you has very nearly, yes, indeed very nearly, cost him his life."

Poor Nellie! she had nothing to say to this; she let the old lady run on, listening while she wiped away the tears that every now and then persisted in flowing. She loved Lady Frankwell, and felt that if she ever did want a mother-in-law she would prefer her ladyship to any one in the world.

The good old lady talked for nearly twenty minutes, and the peroration of her speech ran thus :—

"Well, Fenella dear, when you see my poor pale handsome son, your naughty little hard heart will melt."

"Dear Lady Frankwell, I am not hard-hearted."

"No, my child, you are not. There [a kiss], now run upstairs and put your hat on."

Nellie ran up. She was a mass of confused sensations, and all she knew was that she had consented to go with Lady Frankwell to see Sir Harry, and that she had promised to try to soothe him by talking kindly, feelingly, and cheerfully.

To do this would require, under the circumstances, more courage than had been necessary for the elopement.

Whilst he was in bed, Sir Harry kept himself quiet enough, upset though he was in mind, but when he got up to-day, despite his weakness, he found a quiet life entirely out of the question. In a moment the bitterness of that cruel refusal, and the awful blank it left, racked and excited him.   He got up from the sofa as if demoniacally possessed, and then began walking up and down the room at furious pace, gesticulating and throwing himself about.   He felt thoroughly broken-hearted, thoroughly overwhelmed by the intensity of his trouble, and his life seemed at the moment as if it were without aim or object, as if its vitality were crushed and gone.

For three or four minutes this fresh attack of exhausting excitement lasted, and then, thoroughly overcome, for he was very weak, he fell down at full length upon the floor.

Lady Frankwell and Nellie said very little as they walked from Church Street to the East Parade.

Nellie felt nervous.   She would not know what on earth to say to Sir Harry when she saw him. It was impossible to help sympathising with him, and sympathy is love if you give it its head ; she did not want to love him, or rather, she did not want to increase the affection she felt for him at the present moment.   She loved him above all other men in the world, but for all that she did not want to marry him. She was evidently anything but a "confirmed" widow !   There is no saying now, however, what time may bring about.

Lady Frankwell and Nellie walked somewhat quickly to the poor lover's lodgings, and came into the room a minute or two after he had fallen upon the floor.

His eyes were closed, his face white and ghost like.

To his mother he seemed insensible.

To Nellie—dead !

CHAPTER XV.

NELLIE LORFORD PROPOSES!

NELLIE LORFORD was not one of those women, so truly pitiable, whose lamentable timidity can proceed from nothing but weakness of intellect; yet, though she neither shrieked nor fainted, she was painfully nervous, and much overcome by the sight before her.

She believed Sir Harry dead, and well therefore might she be startled into nervousness and anxious fear. She instantly turned to Lady Frankwell.

"Don't fear, my child, don't fear," said the old lady in a low gentle voice; "I have seen poor Harry in this way before. Ring the bell, dear, and then I think you had better leave us, for Harry would be fearfully excited if he saw you."

"Oh! Lady Frankwell, Sir Harry cannot be in this state because— because—" of me she was going to say.

"Because you refused him; yes, dear, because you refused him," replied her ladyship plumply. "But we will not talk of that now; that is a rent which can very soon be mended; ring the bell, my dear, and then run away."

"Let me, Lady Frankwell, let me and no one else, go for Mr. Reade, the doctor; do let me."

"No, dear; ring the bell directly, and then go. See, he is opening his eyes; go, Fenella, at once."

It was with difficulty that Nellie could bring

herself to leave; but go she did, for go she felt she must. Nothing, however, should prevent her going for Mr. Reade, and off she went, being overtaken in the last fifty yards by Lady Frankwell's footman, bound for the same port as herself.

"Was the doctor at home?" she asked on seeing the man, a minute after, come from the house.

"No, ma'am."

Poor Nellie! she felt ready to cry, but she did something better than that: she told the footman the address of another doctor, and went off straight to a third herself.

Hardly had she gone fifty yards before she descried Mr. Reade hurrying towards the station.

How she ran! She could not have gone faster had there been a buffalo at her heels; and how men, women, and children stared at her!

She caught the doctor just as he entered the station; and when at length she could recover enough breath wherewith to speak, she told her mission, implored him to miss his train, and, when he consented, insisted upon sending him off flying in a basket-carriage.

Then Nellie felt comparatively happy, for she had done what she could for Sir Harry. Now she might think of herself; now she might rest and try to quiet and calm herself; for, what with anxiety, nervousness, and running, she was thoroughly exhausted.

Sir Harry, as we are aware, was out of order both in mind and body, and perfect rest, with medical and nursing care, had some difficulty in putting him straight even in a fortnight's time.

Of course his swift-footed friend Nellie saw him not during that time, but she daily heard of him from Lady Frankwell.

These were trying times for the Guardsman, for he was most desperately smitten, the lovely widow seeming trebly lovely after the separation of a few days. Sometimes Gilbert escorted her home, and sometimes he would play with the boys, the elder of whom one day rather unpleasantly observed to him, "I like the other Misser Frankwell better than 'ou, and so does mama."

But neither by word nor deed, nor even by look, did Gilbert betray his secret to Nellie. He tried hard to read her heart in her eyes, and there were times when hope whispered loudly to him, telling him that if either brother won her, it would be the younger.

It was the intention, however, of the younger Richmond not to show himself openly in the field until the elder had been completely driven out.

Sir Harry's mind tried very hard to delay the recovery of his body, for he would think of the pretty widow and fret himself about her. Nature, however, and the doctor won, as I have before said, and in about a fortnight, the young M.P was out of doors trying not to enjoy a quiet drive in a basket-carriage. He was too weak to tool the immortal Conservative drag.

"What's the use of trying to prolong my life, mother dear? it is only refined cruelty to an animal. I cannot live, much less enjoy life, without that cruel girl, Nellie. Why on earth did she refuse me?"

"Because she was very foolish."

"Oh! no, mother; there's no folly in Nellie's composition; she has a precious lot more sense than I have. She can't think it wrong to marry again, can she? If she does, I wish you'd find out that chapter in which widows are recommended to marry again. I am sure I remember hearing something of the kind read out four or five Sundays ago."

"Well, Harry, I maintain that Fenella was very foolish; but I have very little doubt that she is much wiser now."

"Well, I shall never dare to propose to her again."

"You will not, Harry?"

"No, I've been bitten worse than most fellows in the proposing line, and I'm getting shy. A third refusal would send me to a madhouse, and I'll not propose to Nellie again, nor to any woman under the sun."

"She might not refuse you again, my dear Harry."

"I won't run the risk, dear mother; nothing hazard, nothing lose, I think you said a short time ago."

"And don't you love her as you used?"

"Ten billion times more than ever, and I must marry her; by Jove, yes, I must. She must propose to me, or you, dear mother, must act for me; for, hang me if I make a fool of myself again."

On returning from his drive, Sir Harry laid himself down on a sofa in the dining-room, and presently he heard a soft musical voice in the passage, and a sound as of fairy foot-falls. Could Nellie be in the house? He listened.

> She is coming, my own, my sweet;
>   Were it ever so airy a tread,
> My heart would hear her and beat,
>   Were it earth in an earthy bed;
> My dust would hear her and beat,
>   Had I lain for a century dead;
> Would start and tremble under her feet,
>   And blossom in purple and red.

Then all was quiet. He persuaded himself that the voice was one of fancy's creations, and in a little while he fell into a light sleep.

Twenty minutes after he awoke, and, as he opened his eyes, he suddenly started.

Nellie Lorford was standing at the head of the sofa, her sweet face bent over him, her bright eyes looking intently into his face. Sir Harry seemed completely bewildered, and felt unable to say a word.

"Well, Sir Harry," said Nellie presently, in a low, gentle voice, "have I done wrong in paying you a visit uninvited and unannounced?"

Could he have heard aright? Was that positively the superb widow leaning over him?

"Well, Mrs. Lorford, how are self and boys? The olive looks well, how are the branches?"

Somehow or other he felt as if fortune were going to favour him, so he smiled and made himself happy on tick.

"I want to talk about you, Sir Harry, not about my boys."

"I had far rather talk about you."

"Oh! no; I'm a good-for-nothing hard-hearted woman, but withal, a penitent one."

"Penitent! rubbish! you couldn't commit a sin if you carried Satan himself about with you in your pocket. You're a riddle, and I can't read you, and you've riddled me in the sieve of your good opinion, and have let me fall through the bottom. Tell me now, Nellie—I shall call you Nellie as long as my tongue can call you anything—tell me the object of this deliciously unexpected visit. Make the object known very gradually, because I'm horribly weak both in mind and body, and could not stand a shock."

This sentence was evidently spoken with antici-pations of happiness obtained on trust. He felt convinced that Nellie had come to mend the rent Lady Frankwell had talked about.

"I have come to tell you that I am very sorry you have been so ill."

Sir Harry looked at her and made no reply, his tongue itching to say, 'Is that all?'

"You are getting quite right again, Sir Harry, are you not?"

"As right as I can expect."

"Oh! but I expect you to get perfectly right, and I have come here to do what I can to make you a happy, cheerful fellow again. I have come here to say—to say that—to say that I——"

"Out with it, my darling Nellie, out with it, you glorious angel."

How Nellie laughed, despite her anxiety to be a little bit serious! Moreover, she was a bit nervous, and what young lady would not feel nervous, who was about to propose to a young gentleman?

"What a queer fellow you are, to be sure! Well, I came to tell you how cruel it was of me to refuse you the other day, when all the time I knew I loved you ten thousand times more than my own life."

"WHAT? [huge posters if you please, O devil.] What?" almost roared Sir Harry. "What, Nellie, are you going—are you going to——"

"Now, Harry, you must not excite yourself; there, that's what I'm going to do, and you must guess the meaning." Whereupon Nellie bent down and kissed the demi-Bedlamite's forehead.

"Oh! my goddess of goddesses, my darling, darling child," he exclaimed, throwing his arms round her and kissing her. "Nellie, my queen

of queens, you'll make a Methuselah of me, I
shall live to be nine hundred and something,
or was it a thousand? I shall sit up, and you
shall sit by me, or rather I'll lie at your feet,
for I'm not fit to be more than your foot-stool.
But for all that, I'm going to be your husband,
Nellie, am I not?"

Sir Harry was in a state of immense excitement,
and Nellie began to fear that he might suffer from a
relapse, but do all she would she could not quiet
him.

"Nellie dearest, have you any idea why I thought
you refused me?"

Nellie looked at her fingers, and played with a
diamond ring.

"Shall I tell you?"

"Yes: why?"

"Because I thought you were in love with my
brother Gil, who is a devilish deal better looking,
and more sensible than I am."

"Rubbish, sir, rubbish. Your brother Gilbert
could have almost any woman at his feet any
moment he liked, for he is one of the handsomest,
most fascinating, and refined fellows I ever saw in
my life: but he couldn't vanquish me, Harry. He
never tried, but if he had, he would have failed:
and why?"

"By Jove, Nellie, I have no idea."

"Because, you modest, old, handsome lump of
stupidity, because I loved you, aye, a great deal
more than I had any idea of till I so naughtily refused you the other day."

"By Jove, Nellie, you'll kill me if you talk
much more in this glorious fashion."

He longed to ask her why she did refuse him,

but good taste interposed, and he was silent on the subject. He settled with himself he could find that out after matrimony, for then, of course, he could ask anything, and then, most probably, Nellie would tell him everything she had done, said, undone and not done, from her cradlehood to widowhood.

Sir Harry had of late tackled the pretty widow by a new method. Folks in love always adopt a code of signals, and one code begets another, and the lady and gentleman can accordingly read one another as easily as two ships can talk at sea on bunting.

Sir Harry had set sail without his International Code, the second time that he appeared before Nellie as a supplicant for her affections.

He had been most kind to her since delivering her from the London solicitor, but there are two ways of administering kindness. By one way you plainly show that kindness is simply kindness : by the other, that kindness is a series of acts upon wings, all of which are leading up to some distant climax. These acts become Arabian Night Stories, and no sooner is one over than another is commenced, but only just commenced before broken off, and then comes the parting for the continuation of the series.

Love-making is like a three-volume novel—if anything so delicious as the former may be spoken of in the same year with anything so horrible as the latter—and in an especial degree when somebody keeps the third volume an immense time, so that a poor wretch is kept hanging upon the end of the second, until he cares little whether Rufus has already four wives or only one.

Sir Harry's acts of kindness to Nellie did not

N

seem to be leading up to anything : kindness seemed kindness only : each act seemed a volume in itself, a complete story, not one spun out or cleverly adapted to three volumes. He worked by no code, only talking for conversation's and agreeableness's sake, not with looks, a thousand times varied, which lovers mean for signals.

And he had a reason for not making downright love to Nellie, according to the principles laid down by, and common to men.

She was a widow, and a woman therefore who commanded double regard from men. She was surrounded by a species of sacredness to which Sir Harry feared to do violence by hinting in the remotest degree at such a matter as new love. Love was forbidden fruit to Nellie, he thought, and he dared not therefore place any before her. He could laugh, and say widows will be widows, meaning that widowhood was the last thing they wished to keep up, and that they were just as devout worshippers at the altar of the unclad little god as fair maidens : but when he came actually into Nellie's presence, he felt that he must be on good behaviour, that his fun must be bottled and corked down, and that he must treat the pretty one with infinite regard, and respect the sacred dignity of her widowhood.

So, from feelings of delicacy, Sir Harry had not made downright love to Nellie, though all the time as madly in love with her as he well could be.

To a great extent he had misled Nellie : had he made downright love, she would most probably have taken herself off from Rhyl, and not have gone near her admirer until she could feel up to fresh love-making.

Her love for Archibald Lorford was great, almost beyond conception, far beyond expression, and her mourning for him correspondingly deep. But, after mourning him, as one of Nellie's strength of affection alone could mourn, for two years, she was unexpectedly brought into the company of one whose history was mixed up with her own, as was no other man's in the world. After being in this man's company for two months, Nellie felt the thinnest end of the thinnest wedge imaginable, gently thrust into her affections, and before another month had gone, she had allowed herself, in the privacy of secret thought, to admit that, if any man alive could in any way make up for the loss of him who was gone, that man was Sir Harry Frankwell.

Her power of perception very soon enabled her to mark the exquisite delicacy with which Sir Harry made and yet did not make love to her, and this fascinated her immensely. This non-love-making was the very art by which her affections could best be won, and Nellie felt herself gradually getting very much in love with her old, faithful, good-hearted admirer.

But she did not wish for any conspicuous, evident, and *prononcé* love-making at present : such would offend her own delicacy, and at once deprive Sir Harry of a leading fascination. She could not feel otherwise than happy whilst matters went on as at present, whilst negative love-making was the order of the day : it would be for time to evolve from these negations that positive, un-mistakable love-making, which immediately leads up to the Altar.

So far, so good.

But what now of our impetuous, impulsive, excitable friend Sir Harry.

Was he a good subject for negatives? Scarcely.
Were his powers of endurance and of inaction of a
lasting order? No.

What more natural therefore than that he should,
trans-Atlantically speaking, "burst up"?

He did burst, as we know, and in one second
suddenly tore to atoms that thin web of delicacy
with which he had enveloped Nellie and vastly
fascinated her.

He forgot himself one afternoon, or, rather, he
lost himself in the fathomless depth of his love,
and on a sudden impulse he proposed.

She could not accept Sir Harry then: the sudden
breaking of the crust of widowhood that had so long
enveloped her, unromanced her, and a thousand
thoughts and recollections crowding into her mind,
drove love over the hills and far away, and made
her hug her widowhood closely and pertinaciously.

Directly Sir Harry had left her she, woman-like,
began to make allowances for him, for right well
did she understand him, right well did she know
the impulsiveness of his nature and the greatness
of his love for her.

Most miserable was she during the rest of that
day, for she had driven away from her the best
fellow in the world, the one who alone could make
her happy.

During the next day she felt very sorry that fate
had brought her and Sir Harry together so soon
after putting on the weeds of widowhood; she
would have liked to have met him a year hence, or
to have met him now and then, and then to have
been separated again for a while, without any

suggestions of love arising; at the end of this separation she would then have acted as her heart was
bound to prompt her.

In a few days Lady Frankwell called, and Nellie
received her with open heart and arms. Now her
sensations were rather different to those of the pre-
ceding days, and she did not talk to Lady Frankwell altogether in the way that we might have
expected of her. She seemed inclined to excuse
herself, and to justify her refusal. We know how
Lady Frankwell treated her, and how her ladyship
succeeded in bringing her into her poor lover's
presence.

We know what followed, and it only remains for
me to add, by way of telling what is yet untold,
that many and many a conversation took place
between her and Lady Frankwell during the next
fortnight, and that it required but little persuasion
to induce Nellie to pay the poor patient a visit on
his return from his first drive this afternoon, and to
say, in fact, all that was wanted to put matters
delightfully straight.

"By Jove, Nellie, I——"

"No, Harry, I won't marry any one that 'by
Joves;' it is not pretty, to say the least, and, what
is more, it is not proper."

"Well, then I'll swear by Nellie; you can't say
that is not pretty."

"You will swear by nobody at all."

"Well then, Nellie, by nobody at all, I mean
to come with you to Church Street, to see my boys.
But I won't dine off them ; no, indeed, I'll dine off
their mother. Come along, my enchantress, my
animate life-preserver. I'm quite strong enough to

go, I am indeed. Your presence and love make me feel competent to tackle the whole P.R."

As they were leaving the house, Captain Frankwell came in.

" Hollo, Gil, by Jove, I've got a sister for you, at last."

" And I am very lucky to have such a one as this, Harry; thank you for the present." He shook hands with Nellie, and hurried upstairs.

" He is not very ceremonious to-day," said Nellie, surprised at Gilbert's hasty exit.

Sir Harry said nothing, giving the matter, in his usual way, but little reflection. He was convinced that Gilbert had tried hard to supplant him, and that on meeting the lucky one with the prize on his arm, " a little grain of conscience made him sour."

Of course, we know, that Sir Harry did the Guardsman injustice.

On reaching his room, Gilbert's first reflection took the form of a wonder.

" I wonder whether she accepted him from downright love, or because the mother had talked her over."

Dive we not into his thoughts. To detail them all, and accurately to describe the state of his feelings, we should have to write, print, and read six chapters.

Spare we ourselves the six.

He was as manly and stout-hearted a fellow as ever lived, but no more proof against Love's troubles than a girl of eighteen. He made some excuse next day for leaving Rhyl, and when in the evening far away from the Welshman's land, he took out his diary, he felt half inclined to laugh at himself and write, " The specktercal was too much fur me. I

klosed the show and then drownded my sorrers in
the flowin bole." Yet he was horribly cut up, but
verily he was sensible, if seemingly unnatural,
in trying to make light of a very heavy load.

"By Jove, Nellie," exclaimed our friend, after he
had half eaten the boys, " you'll want a *trousseau*,
and we must set London to work at once, or it
won't be ready in time for the wedding. Just tell
me what you'll want—prices be hung—to begin
with, say twelve silks, twelve velvets, twelve gre-
gorys, grenadines, what do you call them? twelve
sarcenets, and——"

It was useless for Nellie to try and stop the en-
thusiast. He would put down in his pocket-book
twelve silks, twelve velvets, &c., until he had fixed
upon a wardrobe which, numerically at all events,
might favourably compare with that of the late
Queen Elizabeth of ruffled memory.

"And they must look sharp, because we shall
want to be married—let me see, Nellie—in six
weeks."

" Six months, my dear Harry, more likely."

"Six months!" exclaimed Sir Harry, "six demons.
No, no, I forgot, Nellie; you are not Bob Howard,
or Fred Lyuge, are you? By Jove, no, I must
always talk to you in my best style, go to a ladies'
school, and pick up mincing and propriety. But six
months, Nellie! really you are trying the patience
of the British lion too far. Why a ship could go
to Australia and back in that time."

" And what if it could, my dear Harry?"

" Ah, when you call me 'my dear Harry,' you
floor me, I'm ironed flat then : there's no confront-
ing you women—you sherry and water drinkers—
when you go in for the feminine, and say something

awfully female-like. Nobody but a woman could say 'my dear Harry' as you said it. No, it's no use arguing with an unreasoning being—at least somebody says women aren't up to reasoning—and certainly, that is to say; well, I want to say nothing but what is loving, you know, Nellie, and— But really six months will never do, because I couldn't stand being married while the House was sitting. I should feel such an awful fool, getting leave to be spliced, and then coming back to get chaffed by Bright or Bernal Osborne. I couldn't stand it, Nellie; a fellow does look a fool for a month or two after his wedding; he can't help it, you know."

"Well, I've no wish to make a fool of you, Harry; suppose we give up the idea of matrimony altogether?"

"What! No, I didn't mean to bellow; by Jove, Nellie, I thought for a second that you were in earnest. Come, Nellie darling, say three months and I'll double the *trousseau*, that's fair; or will you go the best out of three, whether it's six months or two? Now cry; heads two months, tails——"

"You supremely ridiculous creature."

"Ah, when you talk in that way I know I'm safe to win. In three months?"

"Well, perhaps, I'll——"

"Oh, you glorious creature, you double-distilled angel! Don't stop me, I must get to the bell, I must have a bottle of champagne, and by Jove I must have a kiss too."

Sir Harry thought the next three months went slowly on purpose to try his temper; he longed to go up in a balloon to put the sun and moon on! but they did go at last, and then he and Nellie were married.

" Well, Hunty, I don't think she'll bolt this time," he said to his best-man as they were driven off to Church.

Nellie looked comely beyond measure on her wedding-day, for she was a fine bird that set off fine feathers.

" By Jove, Nellie, you'd cut up into fifty brides fifty times prettier that Mary Queen of Scots. You are the Ossa and Olympus of beauty rolled into one, and by Jove that is a roll which will never get stale. Ha, ha, that's very good for a honey-moon joke !"

Beautiful though Nellie Branston looked the day she was to have been married at Allhallows, Pearl Street, four years and a half ago, when she disap-pointed the orthodox parsons, the congregation and organ blowers, to say nothing of Sir Harry and Lord Huntingsdale, she lacked then the grace of form and manner so marked now. She was trebly fascinating in the full blown dignity and finish of womanhood. She was the perfection of elegance and gracefulness, and withal a regal specimen of British solidity and freshness.

She was still some years under thirty, and the only business that time would have upon its hands, for a long while yet, would be to add to and make more complete her womanly dignity and beauty.

She was not, perhaps, absolute perfection ; woman can be almost anything but that, but—

> As Venus herself she was pretty,
> As sweet as a jargonelle pear ;
> She was lively, good-temper'd and witty,
> And oh, she had splendid back hair !

> Her dress was the soul of completeness,
>   Her manners the apex of ease,
> Her voice, in its marvellous sweetness,
>   Enthral'd with a hiccough or sneeze!

"Harry dear, the *Times* does not report your speech in the House last night; it merely says you seconded some motion."

"Exactly so, dear, and to tell you the truth I have seconded about twenty motions this last fortnight. A fellow has only to take off his hat and the thing is done, but those boobies at Dudsworth, called my constituents, don't know this, so of course they think I'm an awfully active and attentive member, and that I'm so deuced sharp that I can speak on every subject under the sun. But I did speak three nights ago, and to some tune, for I flatter myself that I put Gladstone down rather neatly; at all events he made no allusion to my speech when he got up to reply. We were debating the Church Rate question, Gladstone supporting the abolition, I going in a hurricane on the other tack. I argued in this way: I said that if a man is such a confounded idiot as to set up his own opinion against that of all the Archbishops and Bishops in the country, who declare the Church to be the correct thing, why he could hardly complain if he were set down quietly at the gate of a lunatic asylum. But how, I asked, do we Tories want to treat him? Why we simply tell the fellow that he must pay a humbugging rate of twopence or threepence, and then we'll let him think just whatever he likes. If that isn't fair, Nellie, I don't know what is."

POSTFACE.

I HAVE presumed to dedicate this volume to those philanthropic M.P.'s who, a few years ago, tried to save their metropolitan fellow-creatures from the agonies of an intolerable distraction. I am happy to say that Sir Harry Frankwell is going to bring the matter forward early next Session, and meanwhile I pray all philanthropic gentlemen who read, write, or talk in their London homes during the season, to promise their support to the honourable baronet. I understand that he means to conclude his speech with the following remarkable words:— And I say most emphatically, Mr. Speaker, that he who makes one organ-fiend grind where two ground before is a benefactor of his species ; he is, sir. I need say no more, but in order to conciliate the right hon. member for C——, and secure his vote, I will end with a Virgilian quotation,

Tityre, tu patulæ recubans sub tegmine fagi ;

and I will only add, that if there had been an organ-fiend within one hundred yards of that beech-tree, Tityrus would never have lain down under it !
Enough, good reader, *vale.*

Claudite jam rivos pueri, sat prata biberunt.

THE END.